The
Comet's
Curse

A GALAHAD BOOK

The Comet's Curse

Dom Testa

TOR®

A Tom Doherty Associates Book

New York

THE COMET'S CURSE: A GALAHAD BOOK

Copyright © 2005 by Dom Testa

Previously published in 2005 by Profound Impact Group, under the title *Galahad 1: The Comet's Curse.*

Reader's Guide copyright © 2008 by Tor Books

A Tor Teen Book
Published by Tom Doherty Associates, LLC
175 Fifth Avenue
New York, NY 10010

www.tor-forge.com

Tor® is a registered trademark of Tom Doherty Associates, LLC.

Library of Congress Cataloging-in-Publication Data

Testa, Dom.
    The comet's curse / Dom Testa.
        p. cm.—(Galahad ; 1)
    "A Tom Doherty Associates book."
    Summary: Desperate to save the human race after a comet's deadly particles devastate the adult population, scientists create a ship that will carry a crew of 251 teenagers to a home in a distant solar system.
    ISBN-13: 978-0-7653-2107-7
    ISBN-10: 0-7653-2107-6
    [1. Interplanetary voyages—Fiction.   2. Science fiction.]
I. Title.
    PZ7.T287Co 2009
    [Fic]—dc22

                                                    2008035620

First Tor Edition: January 2009

Printed in the United States of America

0 9 8 7 6 5 4 3 2 1

To Donald and Mary Testa
Thanks for the books, always . . .

Acknowledgments

I wouldn't be the first author to agonize over how to thank everyone who helped to inspire, encourage, entreat, and shove. Yes, it takes a good shove now and then, doesn't it? "Thank you" just doesn't seem like enough sometimes.

I owe so much to the many early believers, including Karen Anderson, Greg Moody, Jennifer Estes, Elaine Dumler, Judy Bulow and Beverly Testa. Your support will never be forgotten.

Great editors never seem to get enough credit, but Donna Bauernfeind and Dorsey Moore are incredible.

I am so grateful for the love and spirit of Debra Gano, and I'm happy to know that the world is finally discovering her Heartlight.

My son, Dominic, is only the most amazing young man in the world, that's all.

I am grateful to have a host of true professionals in my camp: agent and gentleman Jacques de Spoelberch, and Judith Briles, as well as Kathleen Doherty, Tom Doherty, and Susan Chang at Tor.

Very special love and thanks to an educator who not only has made a difference in the Galahad series, but who daily makes an indelible impression on the lives of young people in and out of the classroom. HML to you, Jen Byrne.

The
Comet's
Curse

W hat you're holding right now is kind of like the old-fashioned message in a bottle. Poor souls who found themselves shipwrecked on an island would jot down a message—usually pretty simple: HELP!—seal it inside a bottle and toss it into the ocean. The idea being that someone would scoop it out of the water and come to the rescue. The idea also being that this someone would not be a bloodthirsty pirate looking for possible treasure that might've washed up onshore with our poor little castaway.

Except this message in a bottle is different in a couple of ways. First, it's a story and not just a simple HELP! It's full of pretty interesting characters, not the least of which is me, thank you very much. They face danger, deal with issues like fear and jealousy and loneliness—things that make me glad I'm not human—and learn as much about themselves as they do one another.

And although there aren't any true pirates, there are some fairly nasty types.

Second, our heroes aren't on your typical island. This island is made of steel, the size of a shopping mall, and the sea is a sea of stars. They're stranded, sure; but they chose to be stranded here because their only other choice was . . . well, their only other choice was a gruesome death.

Okay, easy decision.

Castaways who have been rescued years later often say that—strange but true—in some respects it's hard to leave the island. It's become home, a place of security in an ocean of fear. And although deep down they want to be rescued, part of them wants to remain nestled within their cocoon. An observer might think the island a prison; the shipwreck survivor sees it as a haven. It's all perspective.

This story has its own island, and its own castaways.

I guess I'm the bottle. The message—or story—is sealed inside me.

I like that responsibility. And I don't think anyone else is better qualified to tell the tale.

So let's get on with it. Let's pull the stopper out of the bottle and see what pours out. I'll try not to interrupt (much), but sometimes I just can't help myself.

1

There are few sights more beautiful. For all of the spectacular sunsets along a beach, or vivid rainbows arcing over a mist-covered forest, or high mountain pastures exploding with wildflowers, nothing could compare to this. This embraced every breathtaking scene. Mother Earth, in all of her supreme glory, spinning in a showcase of wonder. No picture, no television image, no movie scene could ever do her justice. From two hundred miles up it's spellbinding, hypnotic.

Which made saying good-bye even more difficult.

The ship sat still and silent in the cold, airless vacuum of space. It was a massive vessel, but against the backdrop of the planet below it appeared small, a child teetering at the feet of a parent, preparing to take its first steps. Soft, twinkling lights at the edges helped to define the shape which could not easily be described. Portions of it were boxy, others rectangular, with several curves and angles that seemed awkward. To an untrained eye it appeared as if it had simply been thrown together from leftover parts. In a way, that was true.

Its dark, grayish blue surface was speckled by hundreds of small windows. Two hundred fifty-one pairs of eyes peered out, eyes mostly wet with tears, getting a final glimpse of home. Two hundred fifty-one colonists sealed inside, and not one over the age of sixteen.

Their thoughts and feelings contained a single thread: each envisioned family members two hundred miles below, grouped together outside, staring up into the sky. Some would be shielding their eyes from the glare of the sun, unable to see the ship but knowing that it was up there, somewhere. Others, on the dark side of the planet, would be sifting through the maze of stars, hoping to pick out the quiet flicker of light, pointing, embracing, crying.

Many were too ill and unable to leave their beds, but were likely gazing out their own windows, not wanting to loosen the emotional grip on their son or daughter so far away.

The day filled with both hope and dread had arrived.

With a slight shudder, the ship came to life. It began to push away from the space station where it had been magnetically tethered for two years. Inside the giant steel shell there was no sensation of movement other than the image of the orbiting station gradually sliding past the windows. That was enough to impress upon the passengers that the voyage had begun.

Galahad had launched.

After a few moments Triana Martell turned away from one of the windows and, with a silent sigh, began to walk away. Unlike her fellow shipmates' eyes, her eyes remained dry, unable, it seemed, to cry anymore.

"Hey, Tree," she heard a voice call out behind her. "Don't you want to watch?"

"You won't notice anything," she said over her shoulder. "It might be hours before you can tell any difference in the size. We won't have enough speed for a while."

"Yeah," came another voice, "but you won't ever see it again. Don't you want to say good-bye?"

Triana slipped around a corner of the well-lit hallway, and when she answered it was mostly to herself. "I've already said my good-byes."

With the entire crew's attention focused on the outside view, she had the corridor to herself, and appreciated it.

2

The discovery of a new comet usually didn't cause much reaction. Astronomers, both professional and amateur, would make a fuss, but the general population was rather immune to the excitement. What was one more in a catalog of hundreds?

Yet this one was different. A rogue, named Comet Bhaktul after the amateur astronomer who had first spotted the fuzzy glow amid the backdrop of stars, was slicing its way towards the sun, and its path would cross just in front of Earth. Several early reports had sparked a brief panic when some astronomers wondered if the comet might actually be on a collision course, possibly impacting in the North Atlantic ocean. But soon it was confirmed that Earth would instead coast through the comet's tail, an event that might cause some glorious nighttime light shows, but nothing more.

Dr. Wallace Zimmer would later recall that for two days the sunsets were indeed brilliant. The horizon appeared to be on fire, with dark shafts of red light streaking upward. Comet Bhaktul's particles at least provided a romantic setting for couples in love.

The truth was that the particles were providing much more than that. They were delivering a death sentence to mankind. No one knew it at the time. Earth swung through the remains of

Bhaktul and continued on its path around the sun, and life went on without missing a beat.

Seven months later Dr. Zimmer pulled up a news report on the vidscreen in his office in Northern California. Just a blurb, really, but as a scientist he was immediately interested.

The story called it an outbreak of a new flu strain. Not just a handful of cases, but dozens, and—this was what amazed Zimmer the most—not concentrated in one region. Most flu variations began in one part of the world and spread. Not this time. These reports were scattered across the globe, and yet the symptoms were all the same.

The lungs were being attacked, it seemed. The only difference was how rapidly the illness progressed. According to the news story, some people slowly fell into the clutches of this new disease, with breathing difficulties and intense bouts of coughing that might last weeks or months. Others were hit more quickly, with paralysis of the lungs that brought on death in a matter of days.

Dr. Zimmer looked at the clock and considered the time difference on the East Coast. Then he switched the vidscreen to phone mode and dialed up his friend at the Centers for Disease Control in Georgia.

"Not much else to tell you besides what you've read," Elise Metzer said to him. "Of course, hundreds of people have called claiming that it's some form of germ warfare, and demanding an antidote. The conspiracy nuts are having a field day with this."

"What about other symptoms?" Zimmer said.

"Well, we know that it's attacking the lungs. Most every case begins with coughing, and eventually coughing up blood. But there's also been a few mentions of blotchy skin, some hair loss even. That's probably just each individual body reacting differently."

Elise scowled and added, "I don't think the immune systems have any idea what's going on, and they might each be interpreting the attacking agent in a different way."

"Well," Zimmer said, "with only a few dozen cases I can see why there's no real data yet."

"Uh . . ." came the reply from Elise. "That story is a little out-dated now."

"What does that mean?"

"It means that this morning I heard there are already over a thousand cases, and growing."

Dr. Zimmer sat stunned. Before he could speak Elise ended the conversation by predicting that the next news report he heard would be front page and screaming.

3

I used to live in a box. Okay, maybe "live" is a poor choice. I existed in a box. And not a very big box, either. Just a small, metal container with patch bays, microchips and a mother of a motherboard. If you ask me about my first memory, I could tell you, but you'd start to nod off pretty quickly. It's not an exciting tale: a string of ones and zeroes, a few equations, a bazillion lines of code, and a ridiculous sound that signaled when I was "online." The ridiculous sound would have to go. Roy was a genius, but he had no sense of hip at all. Just look at his clothes.

Roy Orzini put me together. He used to say that I was "his baby." If that's true, then I've got a few hundred siblings because Roy put an awful lot of computers together. My oldest brother was born in a cluttered bedroom just after Roy's tenth birthday, and the little genius has been popping them out ever since.

I'll spare you the false modesty, however, and tell you right up front that I'm the masterpiece. The other kids were pretty good; a few of them have worked on the moon, Mars and a couple of research stations around Jupiter and Saturn. But I got the big assignment, the biggest ever. Roy's pretty proud, and that feels good. I'm proud of him, too.

These days I'm not in that cramped metal box anymore. I'm everywhere within the greatest sailing ship ever built, sailing to the stars.

*I like the new digs. I like the crew I'm sailing with. I like the chal-
lenge.*

Roy called me OC-3323. Remember, Roy is a geek.

Everyone else calls me Roc.

Triana sat at the desk in her room and placed a glass of water
next to the picture of her dad. She bit her lower lip as images
of her home in Colorado flashed through her mind, images of
both joy and sadness. Thoughts of her dad came as well, which
brought a burst of pain.

She glanced at the few personal items that dotted the room.
There was little that an outsider could have learned about the
teenage girl from these clues. Essentials, really. One exception
was the picture. Her dad, grinning that grin of his, the one that
confessed to a bit of troublemaking behind the outer shell of responsibility. In the picture Triana was still twelve, riding piggy-
back on him, her arms clutched around his muscular chest, the
tip of her head peering out from behind. His broad shoulders
concealed all but the top of her head and her eyes—those bright
green, questioning eyes. Any grin of her own was concealed, but
the eyes conveyed infinite happiness.

Picking up the picture, she ran her finger around the outline
of her dad's face, looking into his eyes. She wanted to talk with
him. All of the fun times they had shared, all of the adven-
tures . . . and yet it was simple conversation with him that she
missed the most.

Triana finally tore her gaze away from the photo and returned
her attention to the open journal on the desk. Most people had
given up writing by hand in favor of punching a keyboard, but
Triana felt more of a connection the old-fashioned way. There was
something about watching the words flow from her hand that
gave vent to personal feelings she could never imagine on a computer. With items such as notebooks rationed severely, she allowed herself only a few paragraphs a day. It was enough for her.

She scanned the last few lines she had written, then took up her pen.

It's funny how such a turbulent world can look so peaceful from space. I know there are storms raging, wars being fought (still), fires burning, people dying . . . and yet it's as if it's all been sealed inside a bottle, and the stopper keeps all the sound inside. And me out. Earth is subsiding, slowly for now, but will soon become smaller and smaller until it disappears. Forever.

She dated the entry then closed the notebook. After one more glance at her dad's picture she called out to the computer.

"Roc, how are we doing?"

"Are you kidding?" came the reply from the screen. "Did you see that launch? Backed it right out of there without scraping the sides of the space station or anything. I'm sure you meant to congratulate me, but in all the excitement it slipped your mind. Congratulate me later."

Triana had trained with Roc for more than a year, and knew better than to spar with him.

She said, "I'm assuming that means everything is running just fine. And the crew?"

"Well, that's another story. Heart rates are very high, respiration is above normal—"

"Yeah. They're crying, Roc. They're leaving home," Triana said, picking up the water glass. She took a long drink, then added, "By the end of the day things should start to calm down."

Roc was silent for a moment, then answered in a voice so lifelike it was hard to believe it came from a machine. "Although you might not believe it, Tree, I understand what you're feeling. And I'm truly sorry for what had to happen."

Triana couldn't think of anything to say to this. "Thanks" didn't sound right.

Roc waited another minute, then spoke again. "I hate to give you something to worry about already, but . . ."

"But what?" Triana said.

"Well, I wear a lot of hats on this trip, right? Keep the air fresh, keep the gravity close to Earth normal, dim the lights, take out the trash, sweep up at the end of the day—"

"What's the problem, Roc?"

"The problem is with the ship's life-energy readings. They don't add up, and to an incredibly efficient being like myself that is . . . well, it's just not acceptable. They're screwy, and that will make me crazy, Tree. Crazy, do you hear me?"

Triana sat up. "What do you mean? What's wrong with the readings?"

"They're not balanced. As you know, every person on this spacecraft has been accounted for and cataloged by their energy output. Glad I didn't have that job. Booorrrriiiiinnnngggg."

"Roc—"

"Anyway, for a journey of five years it's critical to maintain balanced levels in order to sustain food and life-support systems. You know that."

"Yeah, so what's the problem?"

"Well, there must have been a mistake made before launch. Some of the measurements were either inaccurate or . . ."

Roc paused, as if thinking to himself.

"Or else what?" Triana said. "*Could* they have made a mistake before we left?"

"It's possible, but . . . no, I don't think so. I mean, c'mon, it's so vital to the mission, I don't believe Dr. Zimmer or his little elves could have botched that."

Triana smiled at the vidscreen. "I know you're referring to it as 'the mission' for our sake, and I appreciate it, Roc. No sense in us locking ourselves in this can for five years and calling it a 'desperate last chance' or something. But about this imbalance: what else could it be?"

"Hmm. The experts say that stress could do it. Of course, the experts also said that Barry Bonds's home run record would never be broken, and don't they look stupid now. But with all of the stress this crew has been under, I suppose it might knock things out of whack a little bit. I'll check it out again in a day or two."

Triana nodded agreement. She rose from the chair and stretched, her arms crossing over her head. Leaning back, her long dark hair fell almost to her waist. It was unlikely, she thought, that there had been very many ship commanders in history like her. But because this was no ordinary ship—and such a unique moment in history—convention had gone out the window. A sixteen-year-old girl was in charge. She sighed and turned to leave.

"Tree," said the computer voice from the screen.

"Yes?"

"Not to get too sappy or anything, but I think it is a mission. I think it's the most spectacular mission of all time."

Triana smiled again and walked out.

"Remember, you're supposed to congratulate me later for that very smooth launch," Roc said to the empty room.

I t was a university professor in Japan who solved the mystery.
Nine months after Earth's close call with Comet Bhaktul, and two months after the initial reports of illness, he announced the bad news.

Samples collected from the atmosphere during the pass through the comet's tail revealed microscopic particles unlike anything ever seen before. Something in the gaseous exhaust of Bhaktul had contaminated the planet, and its effect on human beings was fast . . . and fatal.

In almost no time the spread of the flulike disease had escalated at a frightening pace. Scientists calculated that perhaps 10 percent of the population had already begun to show the physical signs, and tens of thousands more were pouring into hospitals every day. It didn't matter where you were. No place on Earth was spared.

News reports began to include stories of people abandoning their homes, their careers, and setting off for a secluded place in the mountains, or to a remote location in the South Pacific. They assumed that the disease was spread from person to person, and if they left densely populated areas they would decrease their chance of becoming infected. The problem was that you couldn't hide. Bhaktul had saturated the atmosphere, and human contact had nothing whatsoever to do with it. Nobody, it seemed, was excluded: rich, poor, black, white, male, female . . . this disease did not discriminate.

That was hard for many people to accept, because now lifestyle wasn't important, there were no risk factors to avoid, and no vaccination was on the horizon. And when the most advanced medical teams on the planet threw up their hands in frustration, it sent a shock wave of fear throughout the civilized world.

Strangely, the illness seemed to spare the children. In fact, there were only a few scattered reports from around the world that mentioned a child suffering from any of the symptoms. Test after test was run on both children and adults, but without any definite answers. All that could be determined was that kids were immune to the disorder . . . until they reached the age of eighteen or nineteen.

If you were older than eighteen, Bhaktul was coming for you.

There were many more questions than answers. What were these particles in the comet's wake that triggered the sickness? Why were some people affected sooner than others? Why not young people?

And how much longer did Earth have?

That question, in particular, led to millions of workers walking off their jobs. The attitude was "Why should I bother? We're all going to die anyway." Society began to break down into two groups: those who wanted to fight, and those who preferred to just give up and wither away.

On the West Coast of the United States, a group of scientists led by Dr. Wallace Zimmer reached the conclusion that an alternate plan should be developed in case no protective vaccination was found. Their plan was radical . . . and not what anyone expected.

"We believe," Dr. Zimmer said, "that there are only two possible measures capable of sparing the human race."

The faces of hundreds of colleagues looked up at him on the stage with wide-eyed wonder. For the past two days they had listened to a parade of experts discuss their ideas on defeating the disease. Now, at the close of the scientific assembly, they were emotionally drained and hopeful for something that could work. All morning there had been a buzz that Dr. Zimmer, a well-respected researcher and scientist from California, would be delivering a speech that would electrify the attendees. Now he had their rapt attention.

His large frame dominated the podium. He stood exactly an inch over six feet, with wide shoulders and a stout neck. Although the lines on his face gave evidence of his fifty-plus years of age, his hair had remained full, even while losing the battle with the gray. He adjusted his glasses and looked out over the crowd.

"The first solution would be to remove or filter the deadly particles from Earth's atmosphere," he said. "As you are aware, we have barely identified the particles responsible for the destruction, and it could be many, many years before we could even begin to understand how to contain them." He looked over the rim of his glasses at the packed auditorium. "By that time, it would be too late."

The silence was grim. Dr. Zimmer leaned forward on the podium. "The other idea is extremely radical, but at least a possible alternative. After careful discussion, we feel that if we can't take the deadly organisms away from our kids . . . we should get the kids away from them."

A gradual low hum of chatter spread throughout the assembled scientists and world leaders. Finally, as the room began to quiet down, a biology professor from Michigan stood up and addressed Dr. Zimmer. "Are you suggesting that we build some sort of bubble or domed environment and stash a group of young people? They'd have to come out sometime, you know."

"Yes, that's right, and to doom the race to living out its existence in small, cramped domes would be brutal," agreed Dr. Zimmer. "We believe the planet's atmosphere could remain contaminated for possibly hundreds of years. For that matter, it might have been altered permanently. People living in a dome might never be able to leave."

"Then what are you saying, Dr. Zimmer?"

"A spacecraft. Or, to be more precise, a lifeboat."

This time the room exploded in sound. Dozens of individual arguments broke out spontaneously throughout the auditorium, and Dr. Zimmer simply folded his arms and waited. After a few minutes order was restored, and a woman from Texas rose to be heard.

"Dr. Zimmer, you're not serious, are you? A spaceship?"

"Absolutely serious, madam. A spaceship. But unlike any other craft ever assembled. I mentioned the word 'lifeboat' and that's exactly what it would be: a haven for protecting the lives of several hundred kids."

A tall, thin man in the middle of the room stood up, and Zimmer recognized him immediately. It was Tyler Scofield, a former colleague and now the science department head at a major university.

"And what would you do with this lifeboat?" Scofield said. "Let them orbit around Earth forever? That's no different than sealing them up in domes."

"No, sir," Dr. Zimmer said. "The ship would be automatically piloted to another world. One that we feel has the best chance of sustaining the crew when they arrive."

Once again the room erupted in sound as the various members of the scientific community argued aloud. During the chaos Tyler Scofield remained calm and quiet, looking up at Zimmer. When the uproar had died back down, Scofield addressed the stage again.

"I'm curious about your plan, Dr. Zimmer. A spaceship, which we don't have, filled with children, who have no idea how to operate the ship, on a mission to a planet or planets that we have yet to identify as suitable for human life. On the surface one would think that you have not put much thought into this. But, of course, I'm sure you have."

Dr. Zimmer smiled at his old friend. If the thinly veiled criticism had come from anyone else he might have been irritated.

But Zimmer and Scofield had worked together for many years, and although they now rarely saw each other, they still communicated from time to time and provided whatever help they could with the other's projects.

"Yes," Zimmer said, "on the surface it would indeed look like a desperate, maybe even hopeless, shot."

The audience sat quietly, listening. Tyler Scofield sat down and waited to hear what his old friend proposed.

"I will concede that the word 'desperate' applies. Is there anyone in this room who is not desperate to find a solution to the Bhaktul problem? Every account that I have heard has stated that our planet has five, maybe six years, before almost one hundred percent of the adult population is affected. I would say that leaves us in a desperate spot.

"But I take exception to the word 'hopeless.' For the same reasons I just mentioned, I feel that this is our best hope. Will we find a cure for Bhaktul Disease within the next three to five years? I hope we do. Will we be able to protect the lives of our children and ensure that they never have to cope with this disease? I hope we can. But I'm also a practical man. What if—as awful as it may be to imagine—what if we don't find a cure? What if, after five years, we discover that we have wasted an opportunity during those many years to save something of our civilization? To at least give mankind the chance to survive somewhere else?"

Dr. Zimmer paused and gazed around at the solemn faces looking up at him. "Do we choose to give up? Do we throw up our hands and say, 'Well, we gave it our best shot,' and just go quietly? Or do we try to save a portion of our history, our heritage, our achievements? I can't believe that our species would fight, scratch and claw its way up to this level, to have achieved so much, to have overcome so many improbable odds, just to give up now. It's not our way. It's not what we owe to our ancestors who toiled so hard. And it's not the legacy that we owe our children.

"So, I will never say that this is 'hopeless.' It's anything but hopeless, Tyler. It's the embodiment of hope."

The room remained silent for a few moments, an uncomfortable break that left Zimmer wondering if he had gotten through to anyone. Then, in the back of the room, one person began slowly applauding. Then, another. Soon, more than half the room was applauding, with many people rising to their feet to cheer him on. Zimmer felt a wave of relief spread over him, and nodded to the assembly, thanking them.

Yet not everyone was cheering. Looking across the sea of faces, Dr. Zimmer could see more than a handful of scientists shaking their heads, talking quietly to each other and gesturing at the platform. He had not won everyone over to his side, nor did he expect to. Most troubling to Zimmer, on a personal level, was that Tyler Scofield remained seated, arms crossed, a grim look upon his face. He was not among the believers, apparently. After a minute Scofield rose from his chair and walked out of the auditorium. Zimmer's heart sank briefly, but within moments his attention refocused on his plan.

Questions came at him with lightning speed. Details were being demanded and he had few to offer. When pressed for at least a rough concept of the mission, Dr. Zimmer explained the idea of a ship that could hold at least two hundred kids, separated into compartments that contained housing sections, agricultural domes, recreation facilities, and more. No, it would not be an easy project, but mankind had run out of time. There was no room left to bicker about cost, either. There could be no price put on the plan or the objective. It had to be done, and it had to be done immediately.

The most pressing need, it turned out, was to design a computer brain that would act as pilot, teacher and adviser.

5

Let's get one thing straight, all right? I'm not a babysitter. These kids are way too old and way too smart to need that. If I'm looking over their shoulders from time to time, it's not to baby them; I just happen to be a natural snoop. A nosy computer, Roy called me. Okay, maybe I listen in sometimes when I should be busy testing the filtering system in the water recycling tanks, but is that interesting? Is it? No, it isn't.

Gap Lee is interesting. A good-looking kid, too. Good athlete. Funny when he wants to be. Smart. Oh, and the coolest of the Council members.

Yes, I do know cool when I see it. Who do you think you're dealing with here?

Anyway, Gap is cool, and one of my personal favorites on the ship. Just don't tell anyone I told you that. Anyone, okay? Especially Gap.

Gap Lee waited in the Conference Room, as usual the first to arrive for the meeting. He sat at one end of the table and looked out the window. It faced away from Earth, a frame filled with stars. Gap was again struck by how many you could see outside the Earth's atmosphere. "One of you is our new home," *Galahad's* Head of Engineering said to the stars. "I hope you're ready for us."

He turned his thoughts to his old home, the one that was falling away at thousands of miles per hour. Soon that speed would increase greatly, propelled by the power of the sun's nuclear wind. After shining down on Gap for all sixteen years of his life, the sun now pushed him away, like a mother bird shoving a chick out of the nest, urging it to take wing and begin its new life.

Gap thought of his early childhood in China, raised as an only child by his parents, both of whom were college professors. An early interest in gymnastics was fueled by his training with a former Olympic champion. By age ten he was being groomed for his own championship run and had caught the eye of China's Olympic committee.

Then, on his eleventh birthday, his parents startled him by announcing that they had accepted an invitation to teach at a prestigious school in America. Within three weeks the family had packed up and relocated to Northern California, settling into a modest home amid large trees and rolling hills. And although his parents were concerned about the abrupt change in his life, Gap immediately accepted the challenge of meeting new people and forming new friendships. It seemed everyone warmed to him as soon as they met him. A year of intense language lessons quickly made him fluent in English, and his school grades reflected his obvious intellect. He kept up his training with gymnastics, keeping an eye on that Olympic future.

The only thing that drove Gap's parents crazy was his affection for Airboarding. Even though he wore a helmet and pads, spills were inevitable. His mother would cringe every time he walked in the door with another scrape, bruise or torn clothing. "You would sacrifice a chance at a gymnastics world record, just for this silly hobby?" she would cry. Gap would always smile, melting her heart, and then kiss her lightly on the cheek. "Gymnastics is what keeps me from really getting hurt," he would assure her. "You should see the other kids." She would wring her hands and walk away, chattering in her mother tongue.

Gap sighed now, alone in the room, thinking of his mother. He remembered her tortured look when he was selected for the *Galahad* mission. He also recalled, however, the look of pride on her face when Dr. Zimmer tapped him for a spot on the Council. While home during his last visit before the launch, Gap sat with his mother on their porch, watching the rain gently fall. The air had smelled so good, so full of life, the way it always smelled during a rainstorm.

"You were born to do great things, Gap," she had told him that day. "I always knew that. But your father and I were sure it would come through athletic achievements, not like this." She had taken his hand and looked deep into his eyes. "Destiny does not always take the path we expect," she said. "Yours has taken a change we could never have expected. But you were ready. And we are so very proud of you."

Gap had slipped his hand out of hers and tightly wrapped both arms around his mother. He still remembered the words she had whispered in his ear during that embrace.

"Your path will change again and again. Do not curse the change; embrace it, and make it work for you."

Gap had begun to sob quietly, the sound masked by the falling rain. His tears, slowly trickling down his face, mixed with the raindrops blown onto the porch by a gust of wind.

He often thought about that moment, and had vowed never to forget his mother's advice: embrace change. As he stared out at the multitude of stars, he knew that change would be a regular occurrence over the next five years of his life. Was he ready to embrace it?

"Do you smell smoke?" came the voice behind him, the colorful British accent breaking his trance.

Turning, he looked up into the face of Channy Oakland, the ship's Activities/Nutrition Director. Channy was dressed in red shorts and a T-shirt the color of a sunrise (Gap wasn't sure he had ever seen her in anything but T-shirts). Her dark skin glistened; her hair was pulled back in a long braid.

"Smoke?" Gap said. He sniffed the air a couple of times, then looked at Channy. "I don't smell anything."

"Well, with you so deep in thought a moment ago I felt sure I could smell something burning," Channy said with a grin. She patted Gap on the shoulder, then sat down next to him.

"Oh, you're quite a comedian," he said. He liked Channy, but so did everyone else. It hadn't taken very long for her to capture the "most popular" tag among the crew. One of two fifteen-year-olds on the Council, she brought a sense of humor to the sometimes bleak atmosphere.

"Where did you watch the launch?" she said, biting into an energy block she had brought to the Conference Room.

"The large observation window outside the Dining Hall. I only stayed for a while, though. It got kinda depressing, I thought."

"Hmm. Well, I'm going back in a little while. Lita said when the night side rolls around you can see lightning all over the place. I guess there's something like a hundred storms going on at any one time, and the lightning is really cool. Wanna go?"

Gap thought about the lightning for a moment, which only made him think again about the rain back home. He shrugged and said, "I don't know, Channy. Maybe. I might be kinda busy."

"Oh yeah, lots of work to do, and we'll only have five years to get it done," Channy said sarcastically. "You're goofy."

"You love it."

She crossed her arms, a smug expression painted on her face. "Speaking of love," she began mysteriously, "would you agree that it's a little early in the game for shipboard romance?"

Gap leaned back and put his feet up on the table. He wanted to laugh at the way Channy wasted no time in jumping into her favorite activity: gossip. Coming from anyone else it might have disturbed him, but somehow Channy Oakland was able to get away with it. He grinned at her, running a hand through his short black hair, which, as usual, was sticking straight up.

"So your radar has already picked up romance? We only launched this morning."

"Oh, I think this has been smoldering for a while," Channy said with a whisper, as if the room were filled with eavesdroppers, when in fact they were all alone. This made Gap grin even more, and he whispered right back to her.

"I am *so* intrigued. Tell me more, Inspector. Just how long has it been *smoldering*?"

Channy leaned over to him. "I think since the moment you met Triana."

The grin on his face disappeared instantly. "What? What are you talking about?"

Now it was Channy's turn to smile. She got up and walked over to the freshwater dispenser. "Can I get you something to drink?"

Gap pulled his feet down from the table and glanced around to make sure no one had entered the Conference Room. "What are you talking about?" he said again, a little more forcefully.

"Oh, come on," she said. "I doubt anyone else has noticed a thing, but you can't get anything past me." She walked back over to the table holding a couple of small plastic cups of water. "You can joke all you want about my 'radar,' but it's true, you know. I can sniff it out faster than anyone." She batted her eyes at him. "It's the romantic in me."

With that, she sighed playfully and handed him one of the cups.

Gap started to speak, stopped, then started again. "I don't know what you think you see," he said, "but you can forget about it. I like Triana as much as the next person—"

"But not very many people *do*," Channy said. "I'm not saying it's her fault; she's just very quiet and very private. She hasn't made too many friends, you know."

Gap toyed with his cup of water. "Her job isn't to win any popularity contests. She's got a lot of pressure on her right now. She's sixteen years old and suddenly in charge of two hundred fifty . . . well, two hundred fifty pilgrims, I guess you could say. I wouldn't want that kind of responsibility."

"Yes, you would," Channy said. "You might not have pushed

for the job, but I'll bet you would have taken it in a flash. You know the rest of us kind of assume you're second in command. That's got to be a nice feeling."

"There is no 'second in command.' That's why we have the Council."

"Yeah, whatever. You know what I'm talking about, though. And don't get me wrong, Gap. I like Triana, too. I know she's under a lot of pressure, and I also know this is her way of handling it. Fine. But think about this . . ."

She paused for effect. "If I've noticed the way you look at her and talk to her, don't you think she has, too?"

Gap didn't answer. He began to roll the cup back and forth in his hands.

Suddenly Channy felt uncomfortable. "Don't worry, Romeo," she said. "Your secret is safe with me."

"What secret is that, Channy?" came a voice from the door. Gap and Channy both looked up to see Lita Marques stroll into the room alongside Triana. Lita's black eyes and Latin American skin spoke of her upbringing in Mexico. Flashing a smile that only added to her already beautiful face, she grabbed the chair opposite Channy while Triana went to the end of the table across from Gap.

"You guys already have secrets?" Lita said.

"Yeah, I promised Gap I wouldn't tell, but I guess it's okay for you to know, Lita," Channy said sweetly. Gap stared at her without breathing.

"See, Gap was a little disappointed that you couldn't see the lines between the states and countries from space. You know, like you see on a map?" Channy winked at Lita, then shot a sly glance at Gap, who was slowly exhaling.

Lita winked back at her and fiddled with the red ribbon holding back her hair. "Fine, don't tell me your little secret. I'll just start keeping a few from you."

Channy rolled her eyes. "Oh, please. You couldn't keep a secret if your life depended on it."

Triana interrupted their exchange. "Where's Bon? It's about time to get started."

Gap looked down the table at her. "We're still a few minutes early. He's probably holed up in his crops. You know, nothing about him screams 'farmer,' but he sure loves that work."

"Well, let's face it, it gives him a chance to be by himself a lot, and that suits Bon just fine," Channy said. "He would love this trip even more if he didn't have to share the ship with two hundred fifty other people."

Triana felt a little uncomfortable with the topic. Although she knew that Channy was only kidding around, she was well aware of the negative vibes that Bon could radiate. In her mind there was no sense fanning those flames so early in the trip. She was relieved when Lita changed the subject.

"Word is getting around that most of the major cities in the world are going to fire up every light they have tonight as a kind of farewell sign to us. Should be quite a sight when the dark side rolls around again."

"One of us should watch it with Gap," Channy said, "so we can explain that whole line thing to him again."

Gap rolled his eyes. "You know, I am so looking forward to five years of your act."

Triana didn't respond. She was ready to leave Earth behind quickly. A light show meant nothing to her, other than more pain, a prolonging of the grief caused by the separation. She knew the rest of the crew felt as if they were celebrities of a sort, grand heroes being given a spectacular send-off. Chewing on her lip, she glanced up to see Bon Hartsfield walk in.

Bon, his light-colored hair hanging down almost to his shoulders, immediately walked to the water dispenser after only nodding at the assembled group. The scowl on his face was familiar by now, in contrast to the bright, toothy smile of Lita. He was a year younger than Triana, the same age as Channy, though his severe expression always painted him older. Strong, if not as muscular as Gap, his Scandinavian good looks were smothered by what appeared to be a permanent sour mood. His pale blue eyes, like ice, reflected little warmth. He took his seat, and Triana looked at the faces surrounding her.

"Lita," she said, "I know you've already had your hands full down at Sick House. Thanks for breaking away for this meeting."

"Well, I only have about twenty minutes," Lita said. "We're swamped with messages from the crew, lots of stomachaches, things like that. Nerves, if you ask me."

Triana nodded. "I thought that might happen after the initial buzz wore off."

"Yeah," Lita said. "Anyway, I left Alexa in charge for the time being. She knows what she's doing, but I don't want to leave her alone too long. It's crazy right now."

Bon finally spoke up. "Well, why don't we get started? I've got work to do."

It took an effort, but Triana managed to keep irritation from registering on her face, even though her green eyes blazed. Things had always been tense between her and Bon Hartsfield, from as early as she could remember. There was no question of his abilities to run the Agricultural Department, or any other department for that matter. Yet his personality had clashed with hers, sometimes leaving her to wonder if he might even be removed from his position on the Council prior to the launch. But it had never happened.

"We've all got work to do," Triana said slowly. "Because this is our first postlaunch meeting, I think it's important that we spend a few minutes to make sure everyone is caught up and feels good about what's planned for each department."

Gap jumped in, helping diffuse the tension. "You all probably know this, but I'll tell you anyway. The ship is running fine. No surprises, no breakdowns. Now that we're clear of the space station and out of Earth's orbit we'll start to really pick up speed. The solar sails are almost completely deployed, the ion power drive is kicking into gear and Roc says we'll be outside the orbit of Mars within the next four weeks. After that we'll accelerate at a faster clip. We'll pull the sails back when we do the gravity slingshot around Saturn, but then it's almost full speed ahead."

Channy Oakland spoke up next. "The crew was lectured constantly about exercise over the last year. But there's a pretty good chance they won't take it that seriously now that we're off by ourselves." She grinned. "I might not make too many friends over the next couple of months, but I'm gonna have to be a drill sergeant until everyone gets into a consistent routine."

"And you've already scheduled a soccer tournament, is that what I hear?" Triana said.

"Well, I can't see why we should wait," Channy told her. "I say get active and stay active. The dance program I suggested looks like it might be a hit. Several girls have signed up. All of these activities might help with some of the nerves and depression that Lita talked about."

"Don't forget about Airboarding," Gap chimed in.

Channy said to him, "Can't wait to show off, can you?"

"Bon, anything to report from the Farms?" Triana said. She did her best to keep her tone the same with him as when she addressed the other Council members. But that was hard for her. Bon could be so frustrating sometimes.

"Everything's fine," he said shortly. "Since Dr. Zimmer insisted we plant the first crops a couple of months before launch, a few things are already set for harvesting. The sun panels are working. We had a problem with some of the water recycling tubes, but we fixed that. All is well. Nobody should starve on this ship for at least the first few months."

Coming from anyone else the comment would have been met with good-natured laughter. With Bon it came out with a sarcastic tint that left the Council quiet. After a moment Lita filled the silence with her own report.

"Like I mentioned already, a few stomachaches, some headaches, but nobody really sick. We'd like to keep it that way until we at least pass Mars, okay everybody?" This *was* greeted with chuckles. "Other than that, I'll just wait for Gap to come in with his first Airboarding injury. Especially since he and the other hotshots are too cool to wear their knee and elbow pads."

"Keep waiting," Gap said, laughing. "How much you wanna bet you'll get a soccer injury before any Boarder walks into Sick House?"

Tree was about to bring Roc into the conversation when suddenly the intercom flashed in front of her. Snapping it on, she could hear wild screams in the background. Someone was out of control, panicking, and if there were words mixed in with the screams, they were unintelligible. Tree was able to make out other voices, apparently crew members trying to calm or restrain the person who had lost it. Cutting through the sound of the screams came the intense voice of Lita's assistant, Alexa Wellington.

"Lita, Triana, I need you over here. We have a sensitive situation." It sounded much more serious than a "sensitive situation," but Triana appreciated Alexa's composure. She looked down the length of the table at Gap, their gazes locking instantly. "We'll be right there, Alexa," she said. "Gap, come with us. Channy, Bon, we'll be back as soon as possible."

Triana reached to shut off the speaker, cutting off the shrieks that sent shivers through all of them.

It was a staggering problem: designing a spacecraft capable of carrying 251 teenagers, plus self-sustaining food supplies, water recycling equipment, medical gear and more. The crew would spend many years in space, traveling at close to the speed of light towards a star that had at least one Earth-type planet circling it. The ship would need to contain all of the knowledge and practical information these colonists would require once they reached these new worlds. It would have to overcome any and all obstacles as they developed along the way. It needed a powerful guiding force.

The scientists in charge of the project gave *Galahad* exactly that; they gave it Roc.

Computers had evolved in stages. The early units were the size of small houses and worked hard to compute mathematical problems. By the end of the twentieth century they were the size of small briefcases and could run entire industries. During the early part of the twenty-first century there was a backlash against computers, partly because they were often replacing human beings and costing millions of people their jobs. But also because of fear.

Research had soon led scientists to build computers that were actually able to think for themselves and talk with their operators. Most people were not ready, or willing, to accept a machine that was their equal (or superior) in mental power. There was talk of literally pulling the plug on the computer industry, and some openly pushed for a return to simpler ways of life. For a few years progress was kept quiet, and discoveries in computer science were sometimes not even announced. The business of designing and building the small "talking boxes" became a secret underground business.

Eventually things changed again. There came a time when virtually everyone on Earth had spent their entire lives with computers, and the fear began to subside. The talking, thinking machines were now everywhere, controlling almost every aspect of day-to-day living.

But the *Galahad* project required much more. It was necessary to install one large, master brain aboard the ship that could oversee the entire project and take most of the pressure off the young space explorers. The machine would have to be in charge of the actual flying of the craft, including navigation and course corrections. It would also be in command once *Galahad* reached the new planets, helping to choose a desirable landing spot and making sure the mission ended as smoothly as it began.

Scientists and psychologists agreed that some type of adult presence would also be necessary. The computer that ran the mission would need to act as a guide to the teenagers on the ship, helping to make decisions that affected the everyday life they would lead.

And it would need a personality, to be seen as something besides a cold, calculating box of blinking lights. The kids would have to feel some sort of closeness to it. All of these demands put an incredible amount of pressure on the scientific team in charge of the computer brain. And to almost everyone concerned, they more than accomplished their mission.

The man responsible for putting the complex machine together was Roy Orzini, a funny little man who laughed all the time and always made the kids feel happy, even when the weight of the mission seemed to be impossibly heavy. His spirit was contagious, and his visits were always the highlight of the sometimes-dreary training sessions.

Roy stood less than five and a half feet tall, and maybe weighed 120 pounds. "How is that possible?" Gap had asked him over lunch one day. "You eat all the time; every time I see you you've either got a sandwich or a box of cookies. Where does it all go?"

Roy's straight face hid his wicked sense of humor. "Do you have any idea how much energy it takes to power this?" he said, pointing to his head. "I've got to keep this monster fueled at all times. My brain is a massive power hog. Always working, Gap, always churning away."

"Yeah?" Gap said. "When will that powerful brain be finished with the talking box?"

Roy raised his eyebrows. "Talking box, eh? Let me set you straight, Mr. Lee. This little creation will not only be able to talk, but will do so in several dozen languages. Not to worry, though; I've already programmed it to use small words when talking to you, Gap, so you'll be able to keep up. Maybe I'll teach it to draw pictures so you don't get too confused."

Gap had to laugh. It was foolish to attempt a war of words with Roy Orzini, and best to surrender if you'd started one.

The computer, technically identified as OC-3323, was often referred to as "Roy's Computer" in the early days, soon shortened to RoyCo, and eventually just Roc. Once spoken, the name stuck. And, much to the delight of the kids aboard *Galahad,* Roc came equipped with a personality matching that of its creator. Roc became as easy to like as Roy, and for more than a couple of the Council members it seemed as if Roy would actually be along for the ride.

Not everyone believed the computer controlling *Galahad* should be so easygoing. Roy's supervisor, Dr. Carl Mynet, felt that the brains of the ship should command a little more respect. When trouble struck (and he assured them it would), the 251 space travelers would need a strong, commanding force to rally behind, not some wispy, wisecracking "best friend." That was no way to toughen up the crew.

"Dr. Mynet," Roy argued, "these are fifteen- and sixteen-year-old kids. They're not marines in boot camp."

"Mr. Orzini," Mynet said, "perhaps you should start treating them more like marines and less like schoolkids at recess. How do you expect them to perform under stress?"

"I expect them to perform rather well, actually. I'm also thinking of the ninety-nine percent of the time when there won't be an emergency, and they'll need a friendly voice. They're leaving their families behind, Dr. Mynet. Two hundred fifty-one teenagers, thrust into a very stressful situation, and with no help other than a computer. That's a tough order."

"It's not going to be a picnic here after they're gone, either," Mynet said. "We won't get a second chance to get this right. Experts now say we've got about six years before the Bhaktul contamination hits one hundred percent of the adult population. And, as soon as our children reach eighteen or nineteen, it will strike them. We can't afford to coddle these kids. They need to know the seriousness of this mission. And some laid-back, fluffy computer is not the answer. *They* need to be tough, so *it* needs to be tough."

Roy Orzini held his tongue. It obviously would do no good to debate the issue with Carl Mynet. His only hope was Dr. Zimmer. Roy was confident that Zimmer would agree with him.

7

Y ou know, couldn't we at least have reached the asteroid belt before the first crisis? Apparently not.

T riana, Gap and Lita could hear the violent screams before
they reached the Clinic. Actually, the designers of *Galahad*
labeled the department as the Clinic, while each of the kids on
board simply called it Sick House. Lita Marques was the Council
member in charge, but even she relied mainly on Roc to handle
most emergencies. No one expected the room to be busy so
quickly.

As soon as they rounded the corner and came within sight of
Sick House, they were able to pick out some of the words in the
jumble of screams. Triana heard someone shouting "I saw him,"
and "turn around, turn it around, we need to go back." The
voice was that of a boy, obviously in a highly excited state. He
didn't sound angry; he sounded frightened.

As soon as she saw him, Triana recognized him as a fifteen-
year-old from Canada named Peter Meyer. But his face was a
dark shade of red, splotchy and sweaty. He was worked up into a
frenzy, and Lita's assistant, Alexa, was right up in his face trying to
talk to him while he was held by two other Sick House workers.

Each was struggling to hold on to one of Peter's arms as he jerked wildly back and forth. Without hesitating, Gap and Lita hurried over and took charge. They helped to secure the screaming boy, and Triana stepped up beside Alexa.

"What happened?"

"I don't know yet," Alexa said, a small trickle of sweat beading her forehead. Her blond hair was held out of her face with a small clip. "He was running up and down the halls, screaming just like this. He broke a couple of windows in the Recreation area before a few guys got hold of him. They managed to get him here, but not without a fight. They're in the next room, getting treated for some cuts and scratches."

Triana looked directly into Peter's eyes, and putting her hands on his face, she steadied him while speaking loudly and forcefully.

"Peter. Peter! Stop it, do you hear me?" She gradually lowered and calmed her own voice, causing the panic in the boy to subside. Soon he was whimpering quietly. "Peter, tell me what happened," Triana said. "What's going on?"

"I . . . I . . . we need to turn around . . . we need to go back," he blurted out between sobs. "We need to . . ." He finally collapsed. The two workers led him across the room and placed him on a bed. Triana and Lita stood on one side, Gap and Alexa on the other.

Triana said, "Peter, I need you to relax and talk to me. We can't help you like this. Now, take a few deep breaths and tell me what's going on."

Peter lay back, closed his eyes for a moment, and soon his breathing slowed a little. The panic attack was apparently over. When he finally spoke, it was almost in a whisper.

"We need to go back. We can't leave."

"Why, Peter?" Triana said. "What are you afraid of?"

"I saw him. He smiled at me. He . . . he talked to me."

Triana and Lita looked up at each other. Neither could understand what Peter was talking about. Lita spoke to the boy in a soothing voice.

"Who did you see, Peter? Who was it?"

He licked his lips and opened his eyes, staring straight up at the ceiling. His voice was still a whisper. "I don't know who it is. He looked familiar, though. I've seen him somewhere before."

"Peter, you should know everybody aboard. Try to remember his name."

He shook his head. "No, he's not one of us."

This time Triana looked across at Gap. He met her gaze, and his eyes were wide. She knew he wanted to say something but instead let her handle the situation. She made a mental note to speak with him later.

"What do you mean 'not one of us,' Peter?" Lita said. "You mean not one of the crew?"

Peter didn't answer. Instead he closed his eyes again and put his hands up over his face. He was still frightened.

Triana placed a hand on his shoulder. "Peter, we can't help if you won't talk to us. Are you telling us you saw a kid you didn't recognize? That's okay, there are two hundred fifty-one of us—"

"No!" Peter yelled, suddenly sitting up. "No! Not one of us! Don't you understand? He was an adult!"

There was silence as the three Council members and Alexa exchanged glances. Then Triana looked back at Peter. "Where did you see this man? What did he look like?"

"I was near the Storage Sections. I was just walking around, looking for a window to see if I could see the moon. I was tired of watching Earth, you know? I just wanted to see something else. And . . . and all of a sudden he was just there. He smiled at me, and I froze. He said . . . he said 'Are you ready to die?' And then . . . he was gone. He just disappeared. But I heard him laughing after he was gone. A horrible laugh."

Triana said, "And that's all you can remember? What did he look like? What was he wearing?"

"I don't know. It only lasted a couple of seconds. He was in the shadows, hard to see, really. I remember he had a beard. But I don't remember anything else."

"When you say he disappeared, you mean he ran off?"

"I don't know. One minute he was there, then he just vanished, like into thin air."

Triana looked down at the shaken boy. "Look, Peter, you need to get some rest. We'll go down to the Storage Section and look around. But everything's going to be okay, right?" When Peter didn't answer, she said it again. "Right?"

He nodded, then closed his eyes again. Leaving Alexa at his side, Triana, Lita and Gap walked into the next room and looked at each other for a moment without saying anything. It was Lita who broke the stony silence.

"Well, it was bound to happen. Severe strain. Homesick, too, I would imagine. I'll be surprised if someone else doesn't crack before too long. It might take a few weeks or months before everyone is completely settled."

Triana nodded and bit her lip. Then she turned to Gap. "I know you had something on your mind back there. What was it?"

Gap took a deep breath and rubbed a hand through his hair. "Well, Lita is right. I was just thinking about a talk I had with Dr. Armistead a few weeks ago. She was doing another one of those tests on me, and we started talking about the mental part of this trip. About how you take two hundred fifty-one kids, throw them into a tin can and push them off into space. No matter how well conditioned they are, no matter how bright they might be . . . some are sure to have problems. It's only natural."

He looked toward the room where Peter was lying still on his bed. "This guy is doing exactly what Dr. Armistead said. He's been trained to do a job that usually would take someone at least twice his age. He's ripped away from his parents and sent out on a mission to save the human race. No wonder he's seeing things. Did you notice he said the man was familiar looking? Dr. Armistead told me about some of the early colonists on the space station several years ago who claimed to see family members floating outside the windows. Floating out in space, but looking in at them."

The thought gave all three of them the shivers. Gap finally shook it off and looked at Triana.

"I guess it's my job to at least check it out," he said. "I'll run down to the storage area and see if maybe I can find something that caused him to have this hallucination. Who knows, maybe someone around there said something to set him off. But I'll have a look."

Lita looked at Triana and sighed. "Well, Tree, you've got your hands full already. No doubt everyone on board is talking about this by now. It was quite a scene. I'm gonna stay with Peter for a little while to make sure he's okay."

"Sure," Triana said. "Let me know how he does. And thank Alexa for handling the crisis." She motioned for Gap to join her and together they walked back into the hallway.

"You better check on repairing the damage, too," she told him. "Let's get those broken windows replaced right away."

"No problem," he said. "I'll be back to the Conference Room in about thirty minutes."

"Don't bother. I'm going to postpone the meeting until tomorrow morning. I have a few questions I need answered right now," Triana said thoughtfully.

8

Wallace Zimmer had several crucial decisions that had to be made quickly. The process of crew selection was underway with Dr. Angela Armistead, a noted child psychologist. Young and energetic, she dove into the work with a zest that immediately impressed Dr. Zimmer. The two of them had spent hours and hours discussing the process of examining and evaluating the thousands of candidates, and the challenging prospect of eventually deciding on the 251 who would make the trip. Almost every country on Earth had nominated exceptional kids, which made the task of selecting the final team a monstrous responsibility. The world would obviously scrutinize the choices, with each finalist judged against the thousands of others who didn't make it.

"I appreciate your suggestions," Dr. Zimmer said. "You know what makes these kids tick, and the changes they're going to experience during the voyage."

Dr. Armistead nodded. "The pressure would be crushing on even a group of experienced astronauts, so we can only imagine what effect it will have on teenagers."

She paused, her face a mask of concern. Then she shrugged and added, "Who knows? Maybe the best thing going for them is that they're *not* experienced space travelers."

They both thought about that for a minute, hopeful that Dr.

Armistead might be right. A young, inexperienced crew essentially meant that Zimmer and his team would have a blank slate to work with.

Zimmer broke the silence by clearing his throat. "Well," he said, "we'll have almost two years before launch. We should know a lot about their mental makeup by then."

Within a few weeks Dr. Zimmer realized that the crew selection was taking most of his time, and other important details were being neglected. It was obvious that he needed to find someone to help coordinate all of the day-to-day activities and act as his personal assistant. With time such a precious commodity, he quickly began to interview candidates.

Zimmer sized up the man sitting across from him and guessed his age to be around forty. A quick scan of the man's résumé, however, indicated that he was closer to fifty, and apparently took very good care of himself. His name was Dr. Fenton Bauer, head of a research center in Atlanta that worked primarily with the study of deep-space living conditions. He had helped to design the new domes currently being built on the moon, and was an expert on extraterrestrial living conditions. Some of his designs had been implemented in orbiting research stations around the solar system. He was married, with one child of his own, a son. He and Zimmer hit it off quickly.

"Your accomplishments are impressive," Dr. Zimmer said. "Honestly, I'm thrilled that you've shown an interest in this project."

"Well," said Dr. Bauer, "it looks like my other developments are going to be put on the shelf. I want to work, and I can't think of a more important task than this one."

They talked about the design of the living quarters, the recreational areas, the agricultural spaces and the life-support systems. Dr. Bauer was a wealth of information, and would be an amazing asset to the team. Toward the end of their interview, he asked about the crew.

"Is it true that no one over sixteen will be on board at launch?

I thought tests showed that Bhaktul doesn't develop until a person reaches eighteen or so."

"That's right," Zimmer said, "but I'm not taking any chances whatsoever. When they leave, they're definitely leaving any and all traces of Bhaktul behind."

Bauer sat quietly for a moment, a gray mask clouding his face. Zimmer stood up, walked behind his chair and leaned on the back of it.

"Since I mentioned the long training period," he said, "let me make something clear right now in case it's an issue for you. I'm not going to mislead you about your commitment. You might not get a lot of time with your family until this project ends. We'll relocate all of you, obviously, to our base here in California, but your days will be brutal. Fifteen, maybe eighteen hours a day will be routine. Are you ready to take on that type of responsibility, given the situation?"

Dr. Bauer sighed and rubbed his chin. "Dr. Zimmer—"

"No, please, call me Wallace."

"All right. My family is important to me, Wallace. But I feel like this is something I have to do. My wife and I have already discussed it. She's very supportive. My son . . ." His voice broke momentarily and he paused to compose himself.

"My son and I are not close. He left home last year and I've only heard from him a couple of times since then. He's living with my wife's parents near Lake Tahoe. I'd like for him to come back home, but . . ." Again he trailed off, this time without finishing the thought.

Dr. Zimmer kept quiet for a moment, and then gently said, "How old is your son?"

"He's sixteen."

Zimmer realized that this meant the boy would be too old at the time of launch, and immediately he understood the pain that was evident on Bauer's face. He decided to change the subject.

"One more thing. You're aware, of course, that not everyone is behind our project. Are you familiar with Tyler Scofield?"

"I know about him," Bauer said. "I know that he's leading quite a publicity campaign to discourage people from participating with you."

"Have any of his speeches raised issues with you?" Zimmer said. "Maybe I can address some of the untruths that he's spreading."

"I don't think so," Bauer said. "Anytime someone proposes something that's never been done before, there will be people who cast stones. Shake their comfort zone, it seems, and they would want nothing more than to see you knocked down. History is full of examples. They operate out of fear, which I refuse to do. I'm comfortable with your plan. And I'd like very much to be on your team."

Zimmer smiled. He ended the interview with the stock statement "I'll get back with you," but in his mind he knew that he had found his man.

Triana Martell, exhausted from the stressful start to the voyage, fell onto the bed in her room. After lying face-down for a few minutes, she flipped onto her back and stared at the ceiling, the small plant hanging from one corner. Then she turned to look at the poster of Rocky Mountain National Park beside her, its collage of bighorn sheep, hawks and elk set against the stunning backdrop of Long's Peak. Her left hand drifted up and gently rested on the poster. She remained that way, quiet, for a full minute.

Then her mind turned to the event with Peter Meyer. The boy had lost himself for a while, and might have caused more damage if not restrained. The crew would indeed be buzzing about it, as Lita had predicted, and she wanted to make sure it didn't cause others to freak out.

"Roc," she called out.

"Yes, Tree," came the response, and the voice pattern of Roy Orzini instantly made her more comfortable.

"Has Lita given you an update on Peter?"

"Just that he's resting quietly," Roc said. "She thinks he'll be okay."

"He scared all of us to death, you know."

"Are you kidding? I was almost the first computer to wet itself."

Triana smiled for a moment before getting serious again. "You heard what he said, didn't you? That he saw an adult down at the storage area?"

"Yes, I heard that. Alexa opened up communications with me as soon as they brought Peter in. I wasn't able to catch what happened in the Rec Room, though. I heard a couple of kids got hurt."

"They're okay," Tree said, "just a few bruises and scratches. I'm worried about Peter, of course, but I'm also wondering what this does to the rest of the crew. If they see one person go off the deep end so soon after we've started, they might get a bad attitude regarding the entire trip. We're gonna be locked up inside this can for a long, long time."

She sighed and rubbed her eyes. "Roc, I've never really asked you this, maybe because I didn't want to know. But now that we're off, I guess it couldn't hurt. What do you think of our chances? Are we crazy for making this trip?"

"Yes, you are. What else do you want to know?"

"C'mon, I'm serious."

"No, Tree, you're not serious. You're shaken up right now, and no one would blame you. It's not like you didn't have pressure on you to start with, and now you've got all the drama with Peter. That's a lot on your plate.

"And here's the best part, Tree: this is the first week. Only about another two hundred sixty weeks to go."

Triana bit her lip. "That's very encouraging."

"Look, my friend, if you think this will be the last crisis, you *are* crazy. This incident is magnified because we've only just launched. Everything is new, everyone's nerves are stretched tight, and then this happens before you can even get settled.

"But over the next five years there will be more conflicts. Remember your psych training with Dr. Armistead. She did a good job of preparing you for the changes all of you will experience over the years, both physically and emotionally. You'll hardly recognize the person you are now. And you'll find that your friendships will change, too. People you are very close to now will not be as close down the road. On the other hand, some people that you barely know now will turn out to be your best friends. That's not unique to *Galahad*. It happens to every young person as they mature. You'll need time and space to think and grow. The difference here is that you can't really run away and hide for very long. You're confined to this ship for a big part of your lives.

"I, on the other hand," he added, "will continue to be the same sophisticated, charming and witty intellect that I've always been."

Triana laughed. "Charming?"

"Extremely. I've got excess reserves of charm that I probably won't even begin to tap for years. You're very lucky to know me. Don't you feel lucky?"

"Sometimes. Maybe not right now," Triana said, the smile still on her face.

"You're obviously tired," Roc said. "Maybe a nap would be good. You'll like me much more when you wake up."

Triana again bit her lower lip, a habit she kept promising herself she would break. Her thoughts returned to Peter's encounter near the storage area. It was true that stress could have played a big part in the episode, but one thought kept bothering her: Gap's story of space station crew members who had believed they were seeing family members or friends floating outside. It was almost always someone they knew, as if their brains were plugging in familiar faces for their fantasies. That didn't seem far-fetched to Triana.

But Peter couldn't name the man he'd seen. The closest he came to it was to admit that the man looked vaguely familiar, but not someone close to him. Did that mean something? *Had* Peter actually seen an adult aboard *Galahad*? And an adult with a beard, a trait that was common many years ago, but today was extremely rare. Well, Gap would be checking in soon after looking around the Storage Section. Perhaps he would shed some light on the event.

Triana yawned, weariness beginning to overtake her. "Oh, anything new on that . . . what'd you call it? Imbalance?"

"Still working on it," Roc said. "In the meantime, if I may make a suggestion . . . ?"

"Sure."

"All kidding aside, I think it would be a good idea if you did try to sleep a little bit. You're not immune from the stress we've talked about, you know. How much sleep have you had in the last week?"

Tree smiled and rubbed a hand through her hair. "We should add another entry to your list of job responsibilities, Roc."

"Oh, and what would that be?"

"Mother hen." But she knew he was right. Wasn't it just like Roc to push the right buttons at just the right time?

"All right, I'll try," she said to the computer. "I don't know if I can, but I'll give it a shot. Do me a favor, though. Wake me as soon as you hear anything new from Lita or Gap. With this outburst from Peter, things might get a little hairy with the rest of the crew."

"I'm on it," said the computer. Within two minutes Triana was dozing.

And Roc was deep in thought.

Lita was sitting in Sick House, tapping a stylus pen against her cheek. Her eyes focused on a glass cube that sat atop a folder. The cube was filled with sand and small pebbles, one of the personal items from her home near the beach in Mexico. Over the last few days she had found herself constantly picking it up and watching the sand slide back and forth, creating her own tide, imagining the cool touch of the wet sand on her feet during a morning walk. In her room Roc was more than happy to provide faint sounds of the surf rushing ashore, an occasional cry from a gull. It was her tenuous link with home.

She had just finished her report on the status of Peter Meyer, and, like Triana, she turned her thoughts to what Gap had told them about the early space colonists. She imagined the ghostly specter of familiar faces floating outside *Galahad,* clawing at the windows to get in, mouths gaping, eyes locked wide open. She quickly shook her head, trying to erase the image, but all she did was succeed in replacing it with an image of the man Peter claimed to have seen. The bearded man with the dark eyes. Another ghost?

For some reason she believed Peter. For one thing, his roommate had told her that Peter was fine when he left the group gathered around the window in the recreation section, hoping to find some other spot where he could see the moon. He hadn't been any more depressed than anyone else; in fact, he was even slightly upbeat. Plus, nothing in his psych file led her to believe he would be prone to an anxiety attack. All in all, a pretty tough fifteen-year-old . . . until he was carried into Sick House, screaming. It was true that some people could camouflage their anxiety, bottling it up until it finally burst like an overburdened dam.

So what did that mean? If she really believed Peter Meyer, then Lita knew that meant there could be an adult somewhere in the Storage Sections of *Galahad.*

As Lita sat thinking about it, Alexa Wellington stuck her head in the open door and tapped on it. "Are you busy?"

"No, come on in. I'm just finishing up." Lita let out a long sigh. "I didn't know what to expect during the first week, but it sure wasn't this."

Alexa nodded, a gentle smile on her face. Her long blond hair had escaped from the clip and was now hanging over her shoulders.

"By the way," Lita said, "Tree and I were both impressed with the way you took charge of the situation in here. You handled it like a total pro."

"Well, it's probably just because Peter was screaming his head off. I was so fired up on adrenaline I just reacted. Dr. Armistead used to call it the 'fire drill.' She said doctors and nurses usually were at their best in those cases because they didn't have time to stop and think. They just jumped right into action. I can't believe it, my first fire drill and we're still inside the orbit of Mars."

Lita looked down at her stylus. "Well, all I know is that we have one big mystery on our hands. I think most people want to write off Peter's actions as some kind of space hysteria."

"But you don't think so?"

"No. I might have at first, but not anymore. Not after going over his file and talking to his roommate. It doesn't fit. But . . ."

Alexa raised her eyebrows. "But . . . ?"

The young head of *Galahad*'s Health Department sat forward and said in a hushed voice, "But if Peter wasn't just wigging out over the launch and leaving his family, then that means he really saw someone down there in Storage. An adult." She paused to let that sink in, then added, "And I don't like that idea any better than him temporarily losing it. In fact, I don't like that idea at all."

Alexa looked off into the distance. "It's creepy," she said with a slight shiver. "But . . . but could that even be possible? Security was so tight, how could anyone have snuck aboard?"

Lita shrugged. "It doesn't matter, really. We can't worry about *how* someone might have gotten on board. If it's true, we'll have to figure out what we do about it."

Alexa stood up. "Well, if you're really convinced that Peter might have seen someone, then you need to talk about it with Triana immediately."

Lita looked up at her and said, "I'm going to have another talk with Peter first. I don't want this to turn out to be a false alarm and have Tree thinking I'm quick to overreact. She needs to be able to trust me during a crisis."

"All right," Alexa said. "But if you still have doubts, don't wait. Part of her trust in you is based on you trusting your instincts. That's one of the reasons you're on the Council, you know."

With that, she turned and walked out of Sick House. Lita sat quietly for another minute, then began softly tapping the stylus pen against her cheek.

10

When Dr. Zimmer first suggested a lifeboat to ferry hundreds of Earth's children to the stars, his original design idea was actually very close to the finished spaceship that became their home. His dream of a ship broken up into various segments, each with a different purpose, came true.

"Why are you calling it *Galahad*?" he was asked countless times.

"Sir Galahad was considered the perfect knight," he would reply, "a member of King Arthur's Round Table. Legend tells us that he had the strength of ten men. And, as the knight who successfully completed the greatest quest of all—the search for the Holy Grail—I find him to be the perfect namesake for our own quest. Call it superstition, if you must."

The ship itself was an engineering marvel, a testament to the skills of many people from many nations. It showed what they could accomplish if they put their petty differences aside for a common goal. This goal, of course, being the most crucial mankind had ever faced.

One deck of the ship housed the Conference Room, Recreation Room, Dining Hall, and various control centers and offices. *Galahad*'s Sick House was on this level, too.

The Engineering Section was close to the bottom of the ship, home to the ion power plant that helped propel *Galahad* through space. The solar sails, used primarily to get the monstrous vehicle out of the solar system, and also available as a backup propulsion source, were managed in Engineering. Shops, tool supplies and emergency gear were located around the perimeter. Gap Lee supervised this section.

The Agricultural Domes, or what the crew simply called the Farms, sat at the top of the ship. Bon Hartsfield's background with alternative farming made him a good choice as head of the department that sported crops of vegetables, grains and fruits. With a couple hundred mouths to feed for at least five years, *Galahad*'s Farms were flush with row after row of specially engineered varieties, each chosen or designed for its toughness and bounty.

The bottom level was broken into two parts. One side was very active, with the gym (or Channy's Torture Chamber, as some had dubbed it) and an Airboarding track.

The other half, usually dim and deserted, was home to the Spider Bays. The small escape craft, called Spiders, were kept ready for any emergency needs outside the ship, but were primarily to be used for transporting the crew once *Galahad* reached its destination.

The mysterious, locked Storage Section was also on this end of the lower level. Hallways that meandered throughout these rooms were almost always empty, unless someone wanted to get away and have a quiet walk by themselves. The doors, sealed and impenetrable, held their secrets locked inside.

But the most personal compartments on the ship were placed on the middle decks. *Galahad*'s Housing Levels were sometimes compared to college dormitories. Dr. Bauer and his group of designers knew that privacy was a luxury they could not afford with so many space travelers packed into such a small area. But they did the best they could, making sure that only two people would be squeezed into each apartment. So, everyone on *Galahad* had a roommate, with the lone exception of Triana Martell. Dr. Zimmer was the one who had spoken up on this matter, demanding that whoever was in charge should have the chance to get away from the responsibility, to unwind in private. No one argued.

Because the apartments would be home for each of these kids for years, the design team spent many long hours visiting with teenagers from around the world in an effort to supply an atmosphere that best suited them. Yet it was important that the housing levels should also be able to adapt, especially since the space explorers were going to literally grow into them. Each of the 251 young people on *Galahad* was going to mature as they rocketed toward the star awaiting them, and the ship would have to accommodate those changes. Roc would, of course, oversee the alterations, and decide when they were necessary.

But almost everyone was happy with the way the project's plans had turned out. Each room was a decent size, with comfortable beds, an entertainment center and private wash facilities. When the final list of teens was selected, they were even allowed to come aboard and, with their new roommate, finish the room off with their own decorations. Some of the kids chose posters featuring famous entertainers, either musicians or actors that they idolized. But most made the same decision as Triana, filling their walls with pictures of Earth, including mountains, oceans, clouds, forests and sunsets. There was no telling when, or if, they would ever see anything like them again. By the time of the launch, *Galahad* indeed looked like a dorm that had just been set upon by hundreds of college freshmen.

All in all, *Galahad* was the most ambitious space project ever conceived. And it had to come together in two years.

But what about this lifeboat's destination? *Galahad* could not be set adrift in space to wander aimlessly. A target was needed, a course selected, a plan put in place. After weeks of information gathering and many heated debates, Dr. Zimmer sat late one night with his assistant, Dr. Fenton Bauer, determined to make a final decision.

The office was dimly lit, the glare of the computer screens

lighting primarily the faces of the two scientists. Dr. Bauer, his long, sad face showing the signs of increasing weariness, rubbed his eyes and yawned. Dr. Zimmer knew that his close friend and associate was beginning to face another strain as well. In the past month Dr. Bauer had shown the first symptoms of Bhaktul Disease.

"Do you want to run the numbers again, or are you comfortable with what we have?" Dr. Zimmer said.

"Well, this is the one, I'm sure of that. I mean, we can run the numbers until we drop, but this is the one."

With two quick clicks, Dr. Bauer brought the image of a yellow star up on a large vidscreen. "This will be their new sun," he said. "Eos. I even like the name."

"The Greek goddess of the dawn." Dr. Zimmer gazed at the screen. "Remarkable, isn't it? *Galahad* represents the dawn of a new human civilization. They obviously can rename it once they get there, but I hope they don't."

"Ten planets in orbit, two of them apparently similar to Earth conditions," Dr. Bauer said. "Eos III looks very encouraging. Eos II may be just a tad too hot. I think either one, however, offers as good a chance as they'll get. They both have water and an atmosphere. And five years is not too bad for the trip."

Dr. Zimmer nodded. "Eos. Home away from home." He looked across at his assistant. "We'll announce it Tuesday at our weekly press conference. For now, though, I'm going to bed."

"All right. I'm going to work out one or two more things." Bauer stretched his arms over his head before reaching down and tilting the screen up slightly. "There will be a million questions on Tuesday, and I want us to have a million answers." He coughed once, then again. Dr. Zimmer knew that his assistant had been doing that quite a bit lately. Before he could say anything about it, Dr. Bauer added, "Tomorrow we should talk a little more with Dr. Armistead about the Council, too. I think the sooner you finalize those positions, the sooner the rest of the crew will learn to start trusting them."

"I agree," Dr. Zimmer said. "We can start on that first thing in the morning. I already can tell that you're uncomfortable with some of the possible choices."

"Oh, I'm sure they're all good kids. But you never know, do you? We've all been fooled by kids who turned out a little differently than we imagined."

There was an awkward silence between the two men. Dr. Zimmer was sure that personal feelings were creeping into Dr. Bauer's work, which was only natural. But he wasn't sure how to address it and still respect the man's privacy.

He decided to take a chance. "Changing the subject, and begging your pardon if this is none of my business . . ."

"Yes?"

"Have you talked with your son lately?"

Dr. Bauer fidgeted for a moment. He rubbed his face and glanced back at his vidscreen.

Zimmer immediately regretted the question. "I'm sorry, that's none of my—"

"No, it's okay." Bauer dropped the hand from his face and cleared his throat. "I, um . . . I had a quick talk with him about three days ago. He knows I'm working on this project now, and . . . well, I guess I thought it might make him proud."

"Yes?"

"It didn't. He's part of the rebellious side, the side that seems to agree with your old friend Tyler Scofield. He asked me how I could devote the last days of my life helping complete strangers instead of my own family."

Dr. Zimmer looked down and shook his head. There were way too many people with that same polluted opinion. It had to be tearing up Dr. Bauer on the inside.

"You're doing the right thing, Fenton," Zimmer said in a soft voice. "You know you are."

"Yeah, I know that." Bauer paused before adding, "Sure."

Dr. Zimmer wanted to say something else, but decided that the matter was best dropped. "Good night, then," he said, and walked out of the dim room, leaving the silhouette of Fenton Bauer hunched in front of the computer.

S o which are you, Swedish or American?"
    Bon Hartsfield eyed the girl who had asked the question. They had finished a long week of classroom studies and were slowly walking across the *Galahad* training complex grounds towards the cafeteria. Bon didn't think much of the girl. She tended to talk more than listen, qualities that would certainly work against her when it came time to pare down the candidates to the final 251.

It was becoming obvious that some of the thousand or so young people gathered in California were almost shoo-ins to be picked, based on their academic and physical skills. Bon Hartsfield was one of those that most people assumed would be making the final cut, and the girl, who sat in front of him in their Friday afternoon physics class, had latched on to him lately. Bon wasn't sure if she was attracted to him romantically or just hoped that she might gain an edge through association. Either way, she had engaged him in conversation after each of their classes together.

"Swedish," he said to her. "I grew up in the farmlands of Skane in Sweden."

"But someone told me that you came here from Minnesota or something," she said. "I'm confused."

Bon sighed. He wasn't very keen on discussing his personal life, especially when he wasn't sure of this girl's motives. "I lived with some of my mother's family in Wisconsin for the last two years," he said.

"Why?"

"I don't really feel like talking about that."

"Oh. I'm sorry, I wasn't trying to pry into your business."

"All right." Bon was ready to end the conversation and more than eager to be rid of her company. "I'll see you later, okay?"

Without looking at her he broke away and headed towards the dormitories.

But now his mind was reliving the last few years like a documentary. His brief altercation with his schoolteachers in his hometown of Hassleholm, followed by clashes with his strict disciplinarian father. On several occasions his mother would step in, arguing with her husband that Bon was in trouble in school because he was bored with the subjects. And he was. From the moment he entered grade school he was years ahead of his classmates. He was reading by the time he was four, writing his own stories by age eight and constantly frustrated by the slow pace at which his public education was moving. He decided his school lessons were hopeless and began his own pace of study. When he neglected his classroom assignments his grades plummeted.

His teachers assumed that he was simply belligerent and a troublemaker and asked his parents for help. His father, a farmer who didn't stand for any backtalk, refused to discuss the reasons for Bon's attitude problems. His answer was simple: get into trouble at school, spend more time working up a sweat in the fields. It wasn't long before Bon resented his father and grew increasingly distant from him.

His mother, on the other hand, could see exactly what was going on. She would spend many evenings after dinner talking quietly with her oldest son about his frustrations. Bon felt that she was the only person in the world he could talk to, the only person who could understand him. More than once he confided in her that his primary wish was to get away, to escape the farm and his father's iron hand.

One day when he was eleven he came home from school to find his father waiting at the door. Bon's first thought was that he had forgotten one of his chores. When he saw the letter from his school clutched in his father's hand, however, his heart sank. Two of Bon's teachers had agreed that the boy had become too much of a distraction for the other students, and were proposing a transfer to a private school where he might

receive more personalized instruction. It was the last straw for
Bon's father.

But rather than punish him, Bon was shocked to discover a
softness in his father's eyes. To this day Bon could recall the long
discussion with his parents that lasted beyond dinner and into
the late evening hours. By the time they had gone to bed, Bon's
future was decided. He would leave within the month to stay
with his aunt and uncle who lived in America, and he would attend an accelerated school. All agreed that the change in atmosphere might help the headstrong Swede find his way.

Now, as he climbed the stairs to his dorm room at the *Galahad* training center, Bon wondered about his family. On his last
trip home he discovered that both of his parents were suffering
from the symptoms of Bhaktul, his mother feeling the effects
most of all. Yet neither would discuss it in depth. Instead, they
both wanted to talk of his future, his potential of joining the
Galahad project and his attitude. Most surprising of all, Bon felt a
reconnection to his father. No longer the gruff, no-nonsense
farm owner, he had realized his own mortality and had softened
because of it. Embracing his teenage son for the last time, he had
actually cried, something that Bon had never seen before. "I'm
sorry," he whispered into Bon's ear. "Please forgive me, son."
Bon clutched his father tightly and wept.

Even now, almost a year later, he felt the power of that moment. Slamming the door to his room, he threw himself onto his
bed and draped one arm over his face. No dinner tonight, he decided. No more questions about his past, either.

On his nightstand a picture of his parents, taken in happier
times, sat submerged in shadow.

11

So by now you might be wondering how I work. I obviously talk to the crew, I run the life-support systems on the ship, I answer questions, and I have a lovely singing voice. If you're a girl, and I'm a flesh-and-blood boy, you're all over me.

But I'm not psychic, and I don't "see" everything that goes on around the ship. I'm busy, man. Give me a specific task and I'll knock it out. Ask me how many minutes until we reach Eos and I'll nail it. Ask me what color underwear you have on today and I'll tell you how many minutes until we reach Eos. Please.

So don't even start with this "Did Peter really see someone?" stuff with me. You and I have the same information, so we'll both have to puzzle it out. The only difference is that I'm incredibly smart. Not that you aren't, but when you can recite the table of elements in twenty-six languages get back to me.

I want to know what's going on just as much as you do. I can do the mental part, but the legwork is a little tough. I got no legs, man.

Gap Lee was kneeling in the hallway in the Storage Section of *Galahad*. He hadn't noticed the object at first; in fact, he had already talked with a handful of other kids in and around the area before walking back to the site where Peter Meyer had claimed to have seen the bearded man. No one else had seen anything unusual, although most admitted they had been occupied with watching the launch when they heard the screams. Gap found one of the first people who had come upon Peter, a shy girl from Spain. She had been frightened at first by his outburst, but had then quickly called for help. All she knew was that Peter had been frantic, yelling something about "did you see him?" and really making no sense at all. "Spooky" is how she described it.

Gap then made his way to the vast storage area of the vessel, a maze of halls and compartments. It was here that the biggest mystery of *Galahad* lay. While every other section of the vessel was open to everyone, a few of the sealed storage compartments were labeled "off limits" to the entire crew, including Triana Martell and the Council. Only Roc knew of the contents, or what was planned for them. A few days before launch, Gap had jokingly sparred with the computer, trying to playfully draw some information from it. Roc played along . . . but without telling Gap anything.

"I don't know, Gap, what do *you* think is in there?" Roc had said. "Or, here's another way to think about it: what do you think you'll really need when you get there?"

Gap had chewed on this. "Need . . . need . . ." he muttered. "A big dune buggy with, like, ten-wheel drive."

"Uh-huh. That's good, Gap. How about a magic carpet so that you can just fly around the planet? I think I'm finished talking with you for today. My chips are worn out."

Later, Gap had told Triana, "It's probably just a big survival pack, and they don't want us screwing it up before we get there. A big box of blankets, gas masks and matches, I'll bet." He'd tried to shrug it off, but inside he was deeply curious, as were the other 250 pilgrims. Five years was an awfully long time to play "what's in the box?"

Gap had strolled up and down the corridors for a few minutes, peeking into the storage rooms that were unlocked, and shining a flashlight inside some of the utility crawl spaces. Nothing. And no sign that anything was wrong.

A large window had interrupted the monotony of the hall-way, the same window Peter Meyer had sought for a glimpse of Earth. Gap leaned an arm against it, and on this rested his fore-head. He stared at the night side view of the planet as it receded, large clusters of lights twinkling silent good-byes. Somewhere down there, he was sure, his mother was contributing to the message. Several quick blinks of his eyes beat back the tears.

He pushed back from the window, took one last look, then turned towards the lift. He'd only taken a few steps when a gleam caught his attention. Something shiny was lying on the floor near the wall. He picked it up, rubbed his fingers over it, then turned it over to see the other side. Standing up, he flipped it once in the air, caught it with one hand and slipped it into his pocket. Tree would want to see this. Whether it meant anything important or not, it was the only clue he had that someone had been walking around down here, even if it was only Peter.

With one final glance in both directions, he left *Galahad's* mysterious Storage Section, whistling softly to himself.

At the same time Gap was making his discovery, Roc was running through the thousands of duties he performed every second. Adjusting the heat in the Exercise Section on the lower level, where ten boys had just gathered for an Airboarding session. Updating the health records for the kids who had been slightly injured during the run-in with Peter. Exchanging data with the mission planners on Earth. Running a test on a water dispenser that had been reported broken in the housing levels. And rechecking the energy levels on the ship, the same life-energy readings that had puzzled Roc right after launch. They were still not balanced, and he was sure it had nothing to do with the stress, although that was how he had explained it to Tree earlier.

Something just wasn't *right*. As part of his last transmission to Earth, he had requested a new calculation based on the number of people aboard *Galahad* and their individual energy readings. Whatever was causing the unusual numbers was probably something trivial, perhaps some minor human error made in the hectic rush to get *Galahad* on its way. But Roc wanted to be sure. In fact, as the heart and brain of the mission, he *had* to be sure.

Roc noticed the gentle breathing of Triana as she slept. Although no one would believe it was possible for a machine to have emotions, he adored her. In the year they had trained together he had developed a strong sense of respect for the young lady from Colorado. He knew that she was carrying an extremely heavy burden of responsibility on her shoulders, something no sixteen-year-old should ever have to know. Could he really "feel" sorry for her? Could he actually "like" someone? Was it possible that Roy Orzini could *really* have left something of himself inside the mass of wires and circuits and connections called Roc?

His computer brain raced through thousands and thousands of duties in the blink of an eye, with a few all-too-human feelings hiding within it.

12

A sixteen-year-old? In charge of a hospital? You're absolutely out of your mind!" The noted surgeon bellowed over the video connection to Dr. Wallace Zimmer during an unusually cool summer day. The launch date for *Galahad* had been set, and now, with less than a year and a half to go, Dr. Zimmer was trying his best to cope with a new problem. Finding the right young people to place aboard the spacecraft was not the biggest challenge. No, he was having a more difficult time with the adults who were being called upon to help prepare each section of the ship. Very few seemed to give the kids much chance in learning all that needed to be learned before they were expelled from Earth. Dr. Zimmer could not disagree more.

"Listen," he explained to the doctor, "if we had another five or ten years to educate and train these young people, don't you think that's what we'd be doing? But we don't have five years; we don't even have two years. We launch in sixteen months."

The surgeon, sitting in his office in Boston, snorted. "Well then why bother with any training at all? I can give just enough advice and training to someone to get them into trouble. They're probably better off not knowing anything and just toughing it out. You know, survival of the fittest, all that garbage."

Dr. Zimmer had heard this reasoning before. It still disgusted him that so many people were reluctant to do everything they possibly could to give these kids the best chance at survival and success. What good could it do to bury your knowledge with you?

"Dr. Duvall, I'm asking you to devote three months to pre paring these kids for their voyage. They won't be able to come back for a refresher course. They won't have us there to check their work. They won't be able to treat it like a game and just 'start over.' They need your help. They need—we need—your valuable experience. Would you please at least think it over?"

He thanked the stubborn doctor again, and disconnected. Dr. Armistead pulled a sheet of paper from a file and was holding it out to the mission leader. Zimmer took it and said, "What's this?"

"It's a profile on the girl I mentioned to you last week. Lita Marques. Age, fourteen. Scored almost a perfect 250 on the Benz-miller Test. And, if you'll notice the bio, daughter of a physician in Mexico. Almost too good to be true. She's practically been raised with cotton swabs and stethoscopes. I think you should have a talk with her parents."

Dr. Bauer, listening to this conversation from his own desk, coughed suddenly, covering his mouth with a handkerchief. A pained look shot quickly across his face, then was gone.

Before he looked at the file Dr. Zimmer stared at his assistant. "Are you all right? You can take off early, you know. I can—"

"I'm fine," Dr. Bauer said. "This isn't even related to Bhaktul. It's just a chest cold."

Zimmer was not convinced, and one quick look into the face of Angela Armistead told him that she had her doubts as well. But the project leader decided not to pursue it. Instead he glanced down at the page from Lita's file. An ideal candidate in most respects, certainly the educational score.

He read aloud. "Lives in Veracruz, Mexico. Father owns a store, mother a doctor. Hmm, and she's a history buff." He looked at Dr. Armistead. "I find that to be an interesting touch, don't you?"

She smiled. "Then you'll love this irony: her particular interest in history? Famous explorers."

A chuckle escaped Dr. Zimmer. "Signs, Angela, signs. I don't usually believe in them, but this . . ." He closed the folder and tapped it with his fingers. "Plus, I can't wait to tell the charming Dr. Duvall that he won't be training a sixteen-year-old to run the hospital on *Galahad* after all. Ms. Marques will still be fifteen when they launch." He tossed the file across to Bauer, who coughed twice and winced.

13

G ap finished his work early in the afternoon. His dinner
break wasn't scheduled to begin for another hour—more
than enough time for a little fun at the Airboarding track.

After a quick stop at his room to change into shorts and grab
his pads and helmet, he raced back down to the lower level of
Galahad, past several of the sealed storage units and into the
room set aside for Airboarding. "We're lucky to have this," he
thought as he swept into the large padded room. Dr. Zimmer
had argued for months that it was a complete waste of valuable
space aboard a spacecraft that didn't have room to spare.

"You already have an extensive Recreation Room, an exercise
facility and—for goodness sakes—a soccer field! A soccer field
inside a spaceship! How in the world do you expect to justify
space for an . . . an Airboard room, or whatever you call it?"
Zimmer had asked the group of boarders.

"It's an Airboarding track, Dr. Z.," Gap had said. "It doesn't
take up *that* much room."

"Are you kidding?" Zimmer had said, trying to keep the exas-
peration out of his voice. "Every square inch is crucial. And for
just a hobby—"

"This isn't just a hobby," Gap responded. "You're always harp-
ing on us to stay active, to not just sit around in space and grow
fat and lazy. Soccer is great, we all love that. But Boarding is

like . . . like the ultimate test of agility and mental sharpness. You know how important that is."

Zimmer had shaken his head. "Maybe I just don't understand it completely. You have one chance to sell me on it. So explain to me exactly how it works and how it will benefit this crew."

Upon hearing this, Gap had grinned, because he knew that Dr. Zimmer didn't have a chance. Gap Lee had been selected for the *Galahad* mission not only because of his athletic prowess, but also his sharp intellect. And he was skilled in debating the merits of things he loved. Including Airboarding.

To begin with, he explained to the scientist how Airboarding had evolved from the age-old sport of skateboarding. For more than a century kids around the world had thrilled to zipping along on skateboards, where the wheels actually touched the ground. But in the last five years a new version had exploded on the scene. Only this one had the rider suspended in air.

It was an offshoot of the work done on antigravitational trains. The twenty-first century had seen the rapid development of trains that glided just above their rails, kept aloft by giant magnets that repelled each other. The trains used magnetic power not only to keep themselves suspended above the tracks, but also to zoom along at speeds of more than two hundred miles per hour. With no friction of steel on steel, the trains were both fast and efficient.

Then it dawned on one of skateboarding's most popular professionals: why not use that same technology for a little daredevil fun? Within a year the world's first Airboarding tracks were opening around the world.

The rooms were usually the size of a basketball court, with padded walls and banked corners. The key to the sport lay under the floors, out of sight. A series of grids, like the rails of a small railroad track, crisscrossed and threaded throughout the room. Each rail carried a strong magnetic charge which could be turned on and off by a computer that oversaw the competition. On the bottom of each Airboard ran a strip of equally powerful magnets, set with the same polar charge as the ones under the floor. Once situated on the board, the rider was kept hovering about four inches off the ground. As he started forward over the invisible track, he had to use feel to figure out in which direction the charge continued. If the computer programmed the charge on the rails under the floor to gradually bend to the left, the rider had to sense where the magnetic boost was fading and alter his course to the left. If he overran the charged rails, his board would topple to the ground, throwing the rider head over heels.

Early Airboarding rooms did not have elaborate rail systems underneath. They generally started with loops, figure eights and a long straightaway. In recent years, however, floor design had created a frenzied mesh of zigzag patterns, sharp turns and even a few ramps for jumping. Since all of the charged rails were out of sight, riders had to become especially sensitive to the differences between magnetic attraction and diminishing charge. One false move meant a spill. The better riders were able to increase their speed, but also risked a more serious tumble when they zoomed out over an uncharged section of floor.

"All right, I understand the concept," Dr. Zimmer had said to Gap. "And it helps our crew how?"

"Airboarding is more than just a game," Gap said. "It takes a razor-sharp mind, and total concentration every second. As soon as you relax you're down. Painfully. So it will keep our crew mentally sharp for this voyage. Remember, the computer changes the grid for every single ride, so no two trips around the room are the same. You've gotta be able to think fast, or you're a goner."

Dr. Zimmer was not fully convinced. It wasn't until a meeting with Dr. Bauer and Dr. Armistead that evening that he finally consented.

"Listen, he's right about the mental aspect," Dr. Armistead had said. "But I think it's more than that. This sport teaches a lot about risk and reward. The riskier players pick up a ton of self-confidence."

"And broken bones?" Zimmer said sarcastically.

"Well, the rooms are padded pretty well. And they all wear pads and helmets. Or at least they're supposed to. But I'm talking about their spirit. We do want an overachieving bunch on this ship, don't we?"

"Hmm," Zimmer had muttered. "Have either of you tried this crazy game?"

"My son loved it," Bauer said sadly. "I can't tell you how many hours he used to spend at the rec center by our house."

The following day Dr. Zimmer had met with the crew members to explain his decision.

"I want you to realize that in order to build an Airboard . . . place . . . on this ship, something else will have to go. So we're going to look at redesigning part of the Storage Section and leaving off some of the . . ."

He didn't get to finish the sentence. The crew had cheered so loudly that he had to chuckle, shake his head and walk back to his office, leaving them to celebrate. "Oh well," he muttered to himself as he walked with his hands in his pockets, "as long as it keeps them sharp on the voyage they can probably do without a few extra storage rooms."

Gap hustled into *Galahad*'s Airboarding room and immediately saw Rico Manzelli, one of the best Boarders on the ship, and easily the crew's craziest daredevil. Rico was flying across the track, his arms held low and slightly out from his sides as he sensed the magnetic power coursing through the rails under the floor. Approaching one of the banks in the far corner of the room, he suddenly shifted his weight and leaned into a hard right-hand turn. For a moment he almost toppled, then righted himself and turned on the speed down a back straightaway.

Gap smiled and waved as Rico flashed by him, and the wild Italian quickly returned the wave. Gap took a seat on one of the bleachers and watched intently. It didn't do any good to try to learn where the track was energized, because it would be a completely different course for the next run. Instead he kept his eyes on Rico's style, the way he crouched forward, then casually shifted his weight back during a fast stretch. Gap used more of his arms than Rico, which some people thought was bad form. All Gap knew was that he was just about faster than anyone, with the possible exception of the guy currently racing around the room.

As he banked out of another turn Rico suddenly pinwheeled his arms and leapt into the air. He had obviously misjudged the magnetic pull and had veered off course. Tucking himself into a ball, he hit the padded floors and rolled several feet. The Airboard flipped once, twice, and then came to a stop. Gap stood up and gave Rico a sarcastic round of applause.

"I'd give you a nine point five for the form, but only a seven for the dismount," he yelled with a laugh.

"Oh, man," Rico said, huffing as he jogged over to the bleachers. "That's the first time it's done such an abrupt cut out of a banked turn. I guess Zoomer has decided we're getting a little too comfortable out there," he said, referring to the pet name the Boarders had given the computer that controlled the underground course.

"Hurt?" Gap said as he strapped on his shiny silver helmet.

"Naw," Rico said, although Gap knew that it was taking all of his willpower to keep from rubbing where he'd landed on his knee.

"Mind if I try your board?" Gap said.

Rico handed over the bright red board with blue stripes around the edges. "Be my guest. Just bring it back in one piece, okay?"

Gap grinned and jogged over to the starting blocks. He positioned the board over the spot where the magnetic power began and felt the board push up onto the air. Climbing aboard using the plastic handles on the wall for balance, he set his feet, pulled his helmet down tight, then pushed off across the floor.

At first he kept the speed fairly low, adjusting to the feel of Rico's souped-up board. It was obviously a fast, sleek model, and Gap knew that it could cost him a few bruises of his own if he let himself get out of control. He felt the magnetic power ebb on the left side, so he shifted to the right until he felt the strong upward push from below. Increasing the speed a little, he approached a banked turn and leaned back slightly. Using a combination of feel and instinct, he glided out of the turn and maneuvered through a series of twists and turns before coming to a stop in front of the bleachers and jumping off the board.

"C'mon, man, turn it up," Rico said. "My poor old mama could ride faster than that."

"Gimme time to get used to it," Gap said. "This thing is like a racehorse that wants to run."

He climbed back aboard and pushed off. This time he let his speed creep up a little, and before he knew it he was sailing along at an incredible clip. Passing the bleachers, he could hear the hoots and hollers of a few more hardy souls who had ventured in for an afternoon run. The cheers injected him with a little too much bravado, and the next thing he knew he was flying off the board, smacking head-on with one of the padded walls. Behind him came roars of laughter as the assembled group stood and dished out the same verbal abuse he had ladled onto Rico.

Grinning, he walked back and handed the board to Rico. Unlike that daredevil, however, Gap's pride did not prevent him from rubbing his shoulder where it had collided with the wall.

"I'll feel that for a couple of days," he said, grimacing. "But I love the board, man. Give me another shot next time?"

"Sure," Rico said, "if you think you can handle it."

Gap slapped him on the arm and, with a laugh, strolled out of the room and down towards the lift, still rubbing his shoulder. Good thing Tree hadn't been there, he thought, then immediately caught himself and shook his head. Why did it always come back to her? It seemed he couldn't go an hour without somehow thinking about her.

It was even starting to affect his decisions about his work on the Council. He felt it important to sit down and visit with Triana about the events that had befallen them after launch, but should he? If Channy had already picked up on his feelings, maybe Tree had also. He imagined himself walking around with a flashing neon sign on his forehead that blinked "I Love Tree." He'd seen other guys his age make fools of themselves, and he wasn't about to do the same. This is stupid, he told himself.

Since it was dinnertime and the majority of the crew was three levels above in the Dining Hall, it was quiet throughout this section as Gap made his way toward the lift that would take him up to his room to change. He rubbed a hand through his dark spiked hair, then again massaged the shoulder that had absorbed the impact with the wall. He felt the bulk and tone of his muscle, and couldn't help wondering if Triana liked what she saw. He wasn't as tall as he would have liked, but still was athletically built. She would . . . He shook his head, suddenly disgusted with himself for this momentary surge of vanity. What difference did it make what Triana thought of him? He had work to do. There was no time to worry about romance, especially now. He had five years or more to worry about that, and Tree wasn't going anywhere.

Ha! Wasn't going anywhere! He couldn't help but smile at the thought. Where could a girl hide from him on a ship the size of an average shopping mall back home? "Idiot," he murmured to himself. "Get your head on straight."

He rounded a corner and found Channy Oakland waiting at the lift. Oh great, he thought. More "Romeo" talk was sure to follow.

"Hey there, Casanova," Channy said. Gap rolled his eyes. Romeo, Casanova, whatever. It was too bad he liked Channy so much; it made it that much harder to hate her. Her lean, trim figure looked chiseled in her bright yellow workout clothes. The dark chocolate tone of her skin glistened, highlighting the muscular cut of her arms and legs.

"Getting in a little late afternoon workout, I see," he said, changing the subject. That was probably the best way to handle her teasing, he figured. Get her to talk about her passion: exercise.

Besides, if he kept reacting every time she needled him, she would never stop.

"Dance class, actually," she said. "Something you should consider, with your gymnastic background." She noticed the sweat still dripping from his hairline. "And you've obviously been Boarding. Don't get so caught up in that game that you forget about your workouts in the gym. I sent an e-mail to everyone last night reminding them of what Dr. Zimmer told us. 'Never stop exercising your body or your mind. You'll need both in perfect shape when you arrive.' Airboarding might work up a little bit of a sweat, but nothing compared to what I'll put you through."

"Yeah, I know," Gap said. "I'll be there first thing in the morning, ready to let you torture me for an hour."

The lift arrived and they stepped inside. The lift system operated only between sections of the ship. The crew members were expected to walk to every destination within the sections themselves. No laziness allowed.

"Oh, and speaking of e-mail," Gap said when the lift door had closed. "Did you see that the Council meeting was rescheduled for eleven o'clock tomorrow morning?"

"Bon told me before I had a chance to see it." She pushed the button for the crew quarters. "Or, as he said, 'Her majesty has requested our presence.' You know, I like Bon sometimes, but why does he have this attitude about Tree? It's very . . . I don't know, very . . ."

"Childish," Gap filled in the blank, wiping at the sweat on his brow. "I thought he might be jealous of her. Maybe he wanted to be in charge. But after a while I noticed that he has a power problem with everyone. He didn't even get along too well with Dr. Zimmer, remember?"

"You know what he told me one day, about a month before launch?" Channy lowered her voice mysteriously. Gap smiled inwardly. Channy loved to gossip. "He said some of the scientists back in Sweden thought Dr. Zimmer was the wrong man to put this mission together. They thought he was too emotionally involved with the crew. Bon said Dr. Zimmer made too many decisions with his heart and not his brain."

"What would Bon know about a heart?" Gap laughed. "Growing up around the Arctic Circle put ice water in his veins." They were laughing together when the lift door opened. Then, they froze.

The wall across from the lift opening had been vandalized with a large red marker. The words screamed out at Gap and Channy, and shock gripped them:

THIS IS A DEATH SHIP!

14

D r. Wallace Zimmer would have acknowledged that he was, indeed, emotionally involved with the *Galahad* project. In fact, the truth was he *loved* the kids who would be placed on humanity's lifeboat. No one in history had carried so much responsibility, the task of preserving the human race . . . and they were teenagers! As he told Roy Orzini and Dr. Bauer late one evening, "It's tough enough being a young adult. Think of the pressure as you mature, not only from your peers, but from yourself. And we're asking these kids to save our species? It's staggering."

He almost felt as if he had adopted the 251 colonists. He tried to spend time with each of them, but he had so many duties to attend to that it became necessary to concentrate on the key players in the mission: the Council. And, most important, the one crew member who would be in charge at launch. He or she would have to be an amazing person, with not only intelligence, but also wisdom. Dr. Zimmer understood the difference between the two.

Months had been spent analyzing the files of possible candidates. So many had the qualities he was looking for: honesty, courageousness and ability to lead. He had known for a long time that Triana Martell might get the nod, but the final decision was among her, Gap Lee, and a girl from India named Sela. Then,

with the launch only five months away, Dr. Zimmer was shocked
by a visit from a tearful Sela.

"I'm withdrawing from *Galahad*," she told him. "I've decided
to go home to be with my family."

He had been too stunned at first to respond, but spent the
next hour quietly discussing the matter with her. Had her family
pressured her into the decision? Was it for religious purposes?
Was she having a problem with the other crew members? Was
she simply afraid of the voyage?

Sela shook her head softly in reply to each question. No, she
told him, she had decided that she wanted to spend her family's
last days with them, not leaving them behind to embark on a
crusade that had only a slight chance of succeeding. Her family
ties were strong, and she had made the decision, not them. And
she would not be talked out of it.

Dr. Zimmer was saddened, but respectful of her wishes. He
was with her to say good-bye as she boarded the flight back
home. He then returned to *Galahad*'s command center, summoned the remaining colonists and announced his decision: Triana Martell would lead the expedition at launch. No changes
would be made for the first three years of the mission. After that,
the crew members could elect whomever they saw fit to command the next three-year step.

The crew was saddened to hear of Sela's decision, but not surprised at Triana's selection as their leader. Tree, as Roy Orzini
had begun calling her, was accepted by them, admired as much
as anyone else among their elite group. But she hadn't made too
many close friends. She was a loner, which was okay with Dr.
Zimmer. He knew that command was usually a lonely perch. As
long as she was able to cooperate with the other Council members and communicate effectively with the crew, she was a perfect choice.

Dr. Zimmer's long, private discussions with Tree told him a
lot about the girl. Born in Indiana, her parents soon divorced and
she moved at age two with her father to Colorado. He worked

very hard at his job as a computer engineer, but managed to spend a lot of time with his daughter. He loved reading to her, and soon saw that spawn a love of books in her. By her seventh birthday she had mastered the connection into the vast computer library banks and was reading everything she could find. She was also a natural athlete, and the father and daughter duo spent endless weekend hours at the park, tossing or kicking around a ball, climbing on the playground equipment or just simply wrestling in the grass. In time, Triana had grown tall and slender, and made her father proud by excelling in the classroom and on the sports fields.

Her relationship with her mother was another story. An executive with a major corporation in Indiana, and a big shot in her preferred political party, Triana's mother made it clear she had no time to spend with her daughter. Work came first, politics second and nothing third. Tree had flown back to spend holidays with her mother in the first few years, but eventually she just quit going. If her mother noticed, she never acted as if she cared. A single phone call once a month was all that she managed to fit into her schedule. In Triana's mind, her mother was nothing more than a distant relative, and the little girl spent her days happy and carefree in the shadow of the Rocky Mountains.

Until that spring day when Triana's father began to show symptoms of Comet Bhaktul's curse. For some people the disease progressed at a slow, agonizing pace; others, like Tree's father, deteriorated quickly. The microscopic particles attacked his lungs and nervous system, and in a matter of days he was taken away from his daughter, locked up within a medical research lab for tests, and studied around the clock. Triana was able to visit him twice a week, but wasn't allowed to enter the room where he remained hooked up to various machines. So little was known about the epidemic, and doctors were unwilling to take a chance with personal contact. Triana and her father had to speak using an intercom, watching each other's tears through a window that separated them.

Four weeks after he was admitted to the lab, all visits were terminated. Triana was forbidden from seeing her dad, and was told that he was unable to talk on the phone. He had now been taken from her completely, and she knew it meant the worst. Her mother called and offered to fly her back to Indiana, although the invitation sounded hollow to the fourteen-year-old girl. When she declined, and instead insisted on staying in Colorado with her dad's best friend and his family, it almost sounded as if her mother was relieved.

The letter from Dr. Zimmer was sent to Triana's school principal. Ms. Velasquez knew what was going on with Triana's father, and had excused her prize student from classes for a while. Falling behind would not be a problem for the incredibly gifted young woman; on the contrary, she could miss a month or more and most likely still be at the top of her class. Elsie Velasquez wished she had a dozen students like Triana Martell.

She found Triana at home, sitting quietly in her bedroom, her feet pulled up beneath her as she sat next to the fireplace. A notebook and pen lay beside her. Ms. Velasquez noticed that the troubled girl was watching a photo gallery on the vidscreen, a snapshot of Triana and her dad at one moment crystal clear, then slowly fading, to be replaced by another picture. The one currently on the screen had been taken at one of the Colorado ski resorts, and featured Mr. Martell in a wickedly funny ski hat, brightly colored with long, flowing tassels drooping down one side. He was crouching in the knee-deep snow. Tree, pictured in the background, was raising a handful of the powder, obviously ready to launch the snowball at him. Both of them were captured in the middle of a laughing attack, and the faces reflected pure, uncomplicated joy. Ms. Velasquez took one look and knew that no father/daughter bond could be closer. She took a deep breath and fought off the urge to cry.

Triana looked up at the school administrator, then reached over and shut off the vidscreen. Slowly, she rose from the soft carpet on the floor, walked toward Ms. Velasquez and, without saying anything, wrapped her arms around the woman. There were no sobs, no tears. Just a painful minute where no words were needed for expression.

Finally, Triana pulled back and looked into Elsie Velasquez's face. "I don't know when I'll be coming back to school," she said quietly. "They won't let me see my dad."

The school principal gently pulled a strand of hair out of the young girl's face. "We need to talk, honey," she said.

They spent the next hour sitting at the dining room table as Ms. Velasquez recited the information contained in Dr. Zimmer's letter. It outlined the plan for *Galahad,* and described the process of selecting five thousand kids from around the world who would be tested endlessly for almost two years. Eventually the five thousand would be pared down to the final 251 colonists who would leave Earth on the ultimate mission. Based on scholastic scores and health records, Triana had already been selected as one of the five thousand, and, with her family's permission, would leave immediately for California and the orientation sessions for *Galahad.*

Triana listened without saying a word. Finally, she shook her head. "I can't leave my dad," she said. "I can't. I know he needs me. Even if they won't let me see him, I know he needs me here."

Elsie Velasquez wasn't going to argue with the bright young girl. She already felt a twinge of guilt, coming to Triana's home while the girl was openly grieving for her father. But she also knew that the offer from Dr. Wallace Zimmer was a onetime chance, perhaps Triana's only opportunity to escape the clutches of Bhaktul's poisonous grip. Part of her wanted to tell the fourteen-year-old, "Look, you can see what has happened to your dad. The same thing could happen to you if you don't take this chance to escape." But there was no way she could do that. Instead, she nodded silently, rose to her feet and pulled Triana close to her. The two of them stood there for a full minute, arms wrapped tightly around each other, and Ms. Velasquez felt the warmth of her own tears begin to spill down her face. She let go, placing a quick kiss on Triana's forehead, and left.

Five days later, in her school office, Ms. Velasquez received a call from the grieving teen. In a quiet, eerily composed voice, Triana told her, "My dad is gone. They told me he died Friday, the day after you came to see me."

"Honey, I'm so sorry," was all Elsie could think to reply. "I am so—"

"Anyway," Triana broke in, "I've been thinking about it, and I want you to call that man about the space mission."

The principal was shaken by the coolness displayed by the young woman. "Have you called your mother to talk about this?" she said.

"I'm not going to call her. She hasn't been my mother for a long time. My dad was . . . was all I had. There's no reason for me to stay here. If they still want me, I'm ready. I'm ready to leave anytime."

15

When Roy Orzini finished programming me, he did something kinda funny. He showed me some movies. Yeah, I know, you might think that's a little strange, but we're talking about Roy here.

Truth is, I'm glad he did. They were all space movies, movies that usually showed how humans might react to strange things they find out there. Some were a little corny, like Forbidden Planet. Some were very entertaining, like Close Encounters of the Third Kind and E.T. Some were deep, man, like 2001: A Space Odyssey. But none of us is an expert on what will happen when trouble brews in the galactic void; we haven't been there yet. Still, the movies at least show us possible human reactions.

Gap knew that I had seen the movies, so of course he had to be Joe Comedian one day and call me R2D2. What a shame the heat didn't work very well in his room the next couple of days. I don't know how that could've happened.

Look, if we don't get to the bottom of this pretty soon there's going to be some real trouble on this ship."

Gap had the attention of everyone on the Council. They sat in the Conference Room for their second meeting, the first one having been cut short by the incident with Peter Meyer. That was old news, however. The latest buzz around Galahad was the menacing graffiti that had been discovered by Gap and Channy. Triana had investigated immediately, but there wasn't much to go on. The red marker that had been used did not match any of the supplies aboard the ship. And, after some quick questioning of the other crew members who had been in the area, Triana figured a time window of about fifteen minutes when someone could have scrawled the message before Gap and Channy happened along.

Triana sat forward and looked across the table at Gap. "You're talking about the effects on the crew." It was more a statement than a question.

"Yes, I am," he said, tapping his index finger on the table. "When Peter freaked out, it was unsettling, but not surprising. And this might sound strange, but I think it actually helped a lot of kids. You know, some of them were coiled pretty tightly when we launched. Maybe his breakdown relieved a little pressure from them, like it told them 'Hey, I'm not the only one.' But this . . ." He stopped and shook his head.

Lita Marques set down her stylus pen and spoke up. "Gap's right. This thing on the wall is different. Now it's someone intentionally trying to scare us."

"And they're doing a great job," Channy said. "I've still got the chills from seeing it."

"The whole crew has a bad case of the jumps right now," Lita said. "I've had three different people ask me if Peter was responsible for this message. I think they hoped he had something to do with it, so they can just write it off as one kid having a breakdown."

"How is Peter, by the way?" Gap said.

"I checked him out this morning and sent him to his room. He seems okay. Actually, he seems more embarrassed than anything else."

"Let's get back to the graffiti," Triana said. "I agree with Gap that we need to find out who's behind this, and quickly. I wanted all of the crew members to relax and get used to their new lives as soon as possible. That's pretty hard to do when someone is threatening your life. At least that's how I interpret this."

"I thought a big part of our selection process was supposed to weed out anyone who might pull this type of stunt," Channy said.

"Ha!" Bon said with a snort. He hadn't said much since the meeting had started, but now he lashed out. "Those tests weren't for our sake. Those were designed to make the people back on Earth feel good about their choices. You know, if you're gonna send a ship full of teenagers off to 'save the race,' then you want to feel like you made good choices, right? If those tests were so reliable, then how come—"

"How come they let you slip through?" interrupted Gap, causing Channy to giggle.

Bon glared at the engineering leader. "Well, yeah. We all know I don't seem like the perfect *Galahad* specimen. So how come I wasn't weeded out?"

No one answered. In the silence, Bon slowly looked around the table at the other Council members. When his gaze settled on Triana he said, "You wanna know why? Partly because Dr. Zimmer knew this Council needed a different voice. But also partly because those tests were soft. It would be easy for anyone to slip through." His mouth became a grim line. "Don't kid yourselves. Any one of us on this ship might have a loose spring that good old Dr. Armistead wouldn't find out about with her tests. Any one of us."

"That's right," Tree said, returning his stare. "It could be any one of us, even someone right here in this room. But I guess I have a little more confidence in Dr. Zimmer and Dr. Armistead than others might. For the most part I think they were pretty good judges of character. I've only questioned their selection process once or twice."

This obvious jab brought silence to the room and the air seemed to grow thick. Finally Lita diffused the situation by speaking up. "I had a few thoughts about Peter's situation. I think they're at least worth talking about."

For a moment it looked like Triana had more to say to Bon, but instead she turned to Lita. "All right. Go ahead."

Lita took a few seconds to collect her thoughts, and then said, "Well, it just doesn't make sense to me that Peter could have imagined what he claims to have seen. It doesn't fit any of his tests, even though I guess some people don't put much stock in those." She looked at Bon, sitting next to her, but there was no reaction.

Tree bit her lip absentmindedly. "What are you saying?"

"I'm saying that maybe what Peter saw was real."

The statement was followed by dead silence. Each of the Council members exchanged glances, until finally Channy thought aloud. "How could that be possible?"

Triana sighed heavily. "Roc, are you with us?"

"I'm in the bath right now. Can you call back later?" came the computer's reply from the speaker.

"Roc . . ."

"Yes, Tree."

"What do you think about that? About an adult being on the ship?"

"Is it likely that an adult has stowed away on *Galahad*? No. But if you're asking me if it's possible, then yes, I would say almost anything is possible. In fact, do you remember our discussion about the life-energy readings on the ship? How they're not in balance?"

"Yes, I remember," Triana said. "Have you figured that out yet?"

The computerized voice of Roy Orzini was comforting, although the message was not. "No. I've had Dr. Zimmer's people recheck all the readings on their end, and we each come up with the same imbalance. What's interesting is that factoring in another person on board would satisfy the equation."

"Meaning?"

"Meaning that the life-energy readings are just barely out of whack. Just enough to account for two hundred fifty two people on *Galahad,* instead of two hundred fifty one."

Again, total silence engulfed the Conference Room. Roc

sensed the quiet and added, "Of course, I'm not saying this is what has happened. I'm only saying the scientific evidence would support Lita's statement."

"Plus," Lita said, "there's the marker pen used in the graffiti. We don't have—or at least we're not supposed to have—that kind of marker on the ship. Where did it come from?"

"Probably the same place this came from," Gap said. He reached into his pocket, grasped the object he'd found near *Galahad*'s Storage Section and tossed it onto the table. It spun for a few seconds, and then shimmied to a stop. The other four Council members shifted their gaze from it to Gap and back again.

"What is that?" Channy said. She picked it up, looked at each side, and rubbed her fingers along the side.

"It's a coin," Lita said.

"A coin?"

"Yeah," Lita told her, taking the object from Channy's fingers. "Remember hearing about the days when people used things like this for money? Before the United States and most other countries started using the credit bank, this is what people used to buy things. This was called a quarter, because it represented one-fourth of a dollar. But who would have brought one on board *Galahad*?"

The question was answered with blank stares. Tree held her hand out and Lita dropped the coin into her palm. The ship's leader looked closely at the markings, with an eagle embossed on one side under the words "United States of America," and the head of George Washington gracing the opposite side. Under the president's bust was stamped "2021." It was dull and dirty looking, which told Tree that this particular coin hadn't been kept preserved in someone's private collection.

"I've seen one of these recently," she mused aloud, to no one in particular. What she didn't say aloud was that she had seen a coin just like this on a newscast just a few months before their departure. She had brought it up with Dr. Zimmer, who had shrugged it off as unimportant. Could there be a connection between that newscast and this artifact discovered in the bowels of the ship? Logic screamed that it was too much of a coincidence, that she was holding a clue to their mysterious guest.

She stared at the rustic piece of history and then shook her head. "Well, anyway, this could be innocent. We've got two hundred fifty one kids on this ship, and it's easy enough to find out if someone brought this along."

"Why would they do that?" Channy said. "We don't even need the credit bank on *Galahad*. What would someone do with old-time money?"

Triana said, "I don't know, souvenir maybe. Good luck charm. Who knows? But I don't want to jump to any conclusions until we find out. I'll post an e-mail to the crew this afternoon and see if someone comes forward to claim this." She tossed the coin back to Gap.

"As far as this incident with Peter Meyer is concerned," she continued, "I want to proceed for now as if it *was* his imagination. I can't see stirring things up with the crew right now any more than they have been. If something else comes up, then we'll start a serious search for a possible stowaway. Any questions?"

There were none, and the meeting was apparently coming to an end. Bon Hartsfield didn't wait for any formal conclusion, and was the first to push back his chair and stand up. He leveled his gaze at Triana and said, "If you were using your head, you'd start that search for a stowaway right now. That coin didn't come from one of us. You know it, and I know it. It was left for us to find. Just like the surprise visit to Peter, and the threat painted on the wall."

He paused, still with the attention of the entire Council. Lowering his voice, but keeping his gaze on Triana, he put a chill into everyone.

"There is somebody on board *Galahad* who does not belong here. And no matter what his intentions, it's obvious he doesn't mind us knowing that he's here. Maybe because . . ."

He looked at Gap, then turned his cold stare back to Triana before finishing.

"Maybe because he doesn't think there's anything we can do about it."

Silence swallowed the Conference Room. Bon slowly made eye contact with each of the Council members, then stalked out the door. Triana was tempted to shout after him, but bit her tongue. It was ridiculous that she allowed his gruff manner to affect her so. As the others stood and prepared to leave, she touched Gap on the arm and said, "Hey, could you stick around a minute? I want to talk to you about something."

Gap's heart jumped at her touch. Again he had the sensation that she could almost read his thoughts, that same neon message blazing on his forehead. "Get it together," he thought to himself. "Don't be an idiot."

Channy and Lita filed out of the room. Channy was quizzing the head of the Health Department about the coin, and seemed impressed with Lita's storehouse of knowledge. Triana heard Lita mention something about "paper money," and then they were out of sight, leaving her alone with Gap. She looked into his face.

"Tell me something, Gap. You used to be pretty good friends with Bon. I need to know if there's something I'm doing to make him especially edgy with me. Does he tell you anything?"

Gap chuckled and rolled his eyes. "Listen, Tree, it's not you. At least, not that he's told me anyway. Bon's just . . ." He paused, looking for the right words. "He just kinda lives his life in a bad mood. You know what I mean? Some people . . . well, some people are like Channy, and then there's Bon."

"Yeah, I remember his confrontations with Dr. Zimmer and those guys," Tree said. "I think Dr. Zimmer treated him like a sparring partner or something. I still can't believe he made the crew list, let alone named to the Council. But I think it's different with me."

Gap shrugged. "I don't know. I guess I don't see it the way

you do. I just see it as Bon being his typical moody, angry, Mr. Unfriendly self."

Tree sighed. "Sorry to bring you into this. I just thought you might have a little information that could help me. We're going to be stuck together inside this ship for a long time, and I'd really like for us to get along, if that's possible."

"Hey, don't worry about it. You're not the first person he's rubbed the wrong way, and I guarantee you that before we reach our new home he might be the first crew member we stop and let off along the way."

Triana laughed. "Thanks, Gap." She turned to leave, then stopped and looked back at him again. "By the way, I wanted to tell you that I'm glad you're on the Council. I don't know what we'd do without you."

Gap still had the quarter in his hand. He reached up and placed it over his eye, squinting to hold it in place like a monocle. "Well, then," he yammered in his best pirate impersonation, "you won't mind if I keep this as a tip, eh?"

Tree burst into more laughter and patted him on the cheek. "Sure, Blackbeard, it's all yours for now. Unless we find the rightful owner." She walked out of the Conference Room.

Gap waited behind, exhaling loudly. "There's only one problem," he thought to himself, letting the coin drop into his hand. "What if the rightful owner doesn't have a ticket to be on this flight?"

16

enetic screening. The term didn't scare people anymore, not like it had near the end of the twentieth century. In those days many people tried to associate it with selective breeding, or the creation of Frankenstein-like beings, when in reality it was simply a human version of preventive maintenance. Once scientists and doctors had learned the secrets of reading the genetic blueprint, it became obvious that the easiest way to combat disease and defects in people was to stop them before they started.

By the year 2025 it had become common practice to examine the gene structure of an unborn child and to repair any suspect areas that might lead to problems after it was born. Many childhood diseases were virtually eliminated, and birth defects became increasingly rare. Those who had at first objected were slowly convinced by the obvious benefits, until soon the only people opposed to it did so because of religious convictions.

The screening process for *Galahad* was perhaps the most intense ever devised. Of the five thousand young people originally chosen for testing, almost two thousand were immediately rejected after undergoing thorough genetic testing. Dr. Zimmer faced an incredible wave of negative publicity when the results were first announced, as many of the families of rejected applicants cried out in anger, some claiming that Zimmer was putting together the beginnings of a "super race" of humans.

"Nonsense," the project leader told the press. "It's not a matter of trying to create superkids. We're simply trying to give these colonists the best chance at survival in a possibly hostile new world. We want to eliminate as many difficult hurdles as we can, and that includes filtering out potentially dangerous physical ailments. If these kids are the last hope of mankind, why wouldn't we want to help them with every means at our disposal? We can't be influenced by bruised feelings. This is far too important."

Another safeguard included the construction of the Incubator. Its real name was the Sterile Environmental Receptacle, or SER, but Dr. Zimmer hated that label. It would house the 251 space travelers for their final month before launch, isolating them from the outside world. They would be watched and tested in the sterile environment, one final precaution that nothing developed in them that could jeopardize the mission. *Galahad's* passengers would all be in perfect physical shape when they boarded, and once they were sealed inside there would be no chance of any Earth contaminate making the journey.

If the scientists were correct, this would mean even the common cold would be left behind, along with other transmittable sicknesses. Dr. Bauer observed how the kids would all be kept safe and warm for the weeks leading up to their departure, and compared it to a hospital incubator. The name naturally stuck, and from that moment on the Incubator was their final stopping point before the exodus.

While the passengers themselves were being shielded from earthly contamination, the process of keeping their vessel completely clean was under way. As each section of the giant spacecraft was assembled in high Earth orbit, thousands of tiny robots scurried from level to level. Many of them inspected the construction progress, double- and triple-checking each joint, each connection, each wiring patch, each nut and bolt. Hundreds of others were assigned the duty of sterilizing the finished product, vaporizing all remains of human contact left behind. When *Galahad*'s young pioneers stepped aboard, it would be as if they had entered a sanitary laboratory.

Wallace Zimmer had a balancing act to perform. He wanted the ship to leave in absolutely perfect condition, with no traces of germs anywhere. Yet at the same time he was determined that the teenagers who would be carried into space should feel as comfortable as possible, a true home away from home, and the thought of a totally sterile spacecraft sounded too much like a hospital. He was counting on Fenton Bauer's experience with extraterrestrial dome design to help.

"I want these kids to feel completely at home," he told Bauer as they sat in the project cafeteria one afternoon. "I'm allowing them to bring several items from home, and they'll each have a hand in decorating their own room. But there's one thing I don't want them to bring aboard."

"Let me guess," Dr. Bauer said. "Germs."

"Right."

Dr. Bauer nodded in agreement before a sad smile washed across his face. "When my son was little he used to call them 'gerbs.' Every time I would tell him to wash his hands before dinner he would waddle down the hall to go 'get rid of the gerbs.' "

He shifted in his chair and looked across at Dr. Zimmer. "I did my best to teach him about 'gerbs,' how to stay healthy and fit. But there's nothing I can do about these 'gerbs,' is there? Washing his hands won't help him this time. Or you or me."

An uncomfortable moment passed, then Dr. Bauer seemed to recover.

"I know what you're looking for," he said. "Zap the germs on everything from posters to pajamas, but keep the ship feeling warm and homey, right?"

"That's right," Dr. Zimmer said. "I don't want them to feel like their things are being zapped. I'd like to keep their personal belongings exactly that: personal. They're going to feel disconnected anyway once they leave, and I'd like for them to maintain their connection to as many personal things as possible. If we treat these items like lab objects, it's just one more layer of comfort that's stripped away. It's up to you and Angela Armistead to make sure there's still a human touch to all of this."

For the next hour the two men changed direction and began focusing on which kids were qualified to lead the various departments. Of all the candidates for the role of Activities/Nutrition Director, Zimmer was particularly drawn to Channy Oakland.

Bright and enthusiastic, Channy was just barely old enough to qualify for the mission, but Zimmer was convinced that she would play an important role after launch. Her mother, a physical therapist, had made sure that she grew up with a healthy respect for her body and the proper nutrition and exercise needed to keep it finely tuned. Channy and her older sister, D'Audra, had also spent many long hours assisting their mother in her clinic in England, mostly working with the disabled.

One summer day, during a particularly hot stretch of August, Channy had begged D'Audra to sneak away with her to go swimming. They had already worked eight days straight for their mom without a day off, and with school beginning again in a couple of weeks Channy had an itch to visit The Hole. Given the nickname generations ago, The Hole was a secluded pond tucked away in the woods just outside of town. For years kids had ditched school, church and part-time jobs to dive into the cool, crystal-clear water fed by a small waterfall. Channy loved it, and after just a little prodding, convinced D'Audra to slip into her swimsuit and run out to The Hole. Her older sister made her promise that they would be back within two hours, no arguing or whining, and off they went.

It would be a day Channy would never forget. D'Audra, two years older and already a terrific role model for her little sis, had been grinning as she started to leap off the rock ledge, fifteen feet over the water, anxious to prove that she could indeed reach the tree limb that jutted out several feet over the pond's surface below. But the smooth surface of rock was now covered with water, small puddles that had collected from the water dripping off the two sisters, and Channy saw D'Audra lose control just as she planted her foot to leap toward the branch. Although it only lasted a split second, Channy would remember the moment in slow motion forever. Her sister reached back to try to grab on to her for support, but instead plummeted down the embankment, striking the rocks at the water's edge.

The doctors had originally said it was doubtful she would ever walk again, with the damage to her spine so severe. But D'Audra had refused to allow that possibility. Channy watched in wonder over the next year as her older sister bravely fought through two operations and countless hours of rehab work. With her mother on one side and her adoring sister on the other, D'Audra took her first painful steps again exactly thirteen months after the horrible accident at The Hole. Sheer determination and strong will had ensured that the doctors would be wrong. She would walk again, and, she confided in Channy one quiet evening, she *would* reach that branch someday. Someday.

But Channy Oakland would not see her do it. Her mother had received a phone call from Dr. Wallace Zimmer.

17

The lights were slowly dimming in the hallways. Because there was no sun to create day and night, *Galahad* manufactured its own twenty-four-hour day. One of the thousands of duties that Roc oversaw, the hallways and meeting places would slowly light up beginning at six o'clock. It would remain bright throughout the "day," gradually fading to twilight by eight o'clock. The ship's designers knew this was necessary to keep each crew member's internal body clock properly adjusted. There would even be a slight change in the length of days as the calendar advanced, a nod to the changing seasons each passenger had left behind.

Another touch, suggested by Dr. Armistead, was the inclusion of sounds. Earth sounds, from an occasional faint whisper of wind to the barely audible sound of crickets during the "night" hours. Roc kept each of these noises in the background, more a psychological blanket than anything else. A comfort zone, Dr. Armistead had said. Sounds of home.

As the evening began on the eighth day, most of the crew had retired to either the Recreation Area or their own rooms. A group of ten, however, had remained in the Dining Hall after dinner, sitting at one of the large round tables. A deck of cards sat untouched at one side; finding a game that ten people could enjoy was difficult, and, besides, conversation seemed more interesting anyway.

At first the mood had been somber as they each quietly talked about home, nods of understanding punctuating each story. They were their own support group, leaning on one another to get through the homesick feelings, the sadness, the pain. When one person expressed guilt over leaving their family behind, nine others could relate, comfort coming in the form of a touch, a soft word, even a knowing look. Gradually the stories took a turn; tears were replaced with a smile. Fond memories began to lift the spirits.

Gap Lee was trying not to laugh. His face was mostly blank, but the corners of his mouth were cracking into a half smile. The last thing he wanted to do was appear insensitive to the story he was listening to . . . but it *was* funny. Unable to hold it back any longer, he broke out in a fit of laughing.

Angelina Reyes looked at him sharply. "It's not funny, Gap," she said crossly.

"I know," he said, taking a breath. "But it is, kinda. I mean, you did kick her in the head, right?"

"By accident," Angelina shot back. "I didn't mean to." But by now the rest of the group had begun laughing, too. They had all wanted to, but until Gap broke the ice they had each been exercising restraint out of courtesy.

"You know, most soccer players try to kick the ball, not the goalie's head," he quipped. This brought even more laughter from the others, while Angelina's face clouded.

"I was *trying* to kick the ball," she said. "I told you, the goalie dove for it at the last second. I don't know why you're laughing. She could have really been hurt."

"But you said she wasn't hurt that bad," Gap said. "You said she was just a little . . . what was the word?"

"Woozy," Angelina said, and for the first time a smile creased her face, too. "They stopped the game for a couple of minutes, but she stayed in and played the rest of the way." She looked down at the table, trying to compose herself, but eventually failing. Before she could stop herself she was laughing along with the others.

"Yeah, she was okay, but man, was she intimidated by me after that. I scored twice in the next five minutes."

More laughs poured out from the teenagers. After the stress from the last few days, it felt good. It felt *really* good.

Mitchell O'Connor, a thin redhead from Ireland, leaned back in his chair and put one of his feet up on the table. He looked at Angelina and said, "So, when our three-on-three soccer tournament starts, should the rest of us wear helmets when you're on the field?"

"It won't matter what you wear, Mitch," she said quickly. "I could score on you all day long."

A collection of "oohs" and "whoas" erupted around the table. Mitchell put his head back and laughed the hardest. He loved a good challenge, especially on the soccer field.

The whole crew was excited about the tournament. Not only did it provide the needed exercise, but also it drew everyone together in a spirit of teamwork. During their months of preparation on Earth they had held two such tourneys, and each one seemed to strengthen the connections they shared with each other. Dr. Zimmer was thrilled, and let Channy know that her idea was terrific. He encouraged the crew to make these competitive matches a regular part of their lives. He approved of anything to keep a couple hundred kids on their toes during the long, tedious journey.

He had reluctantly accepted their demand for the state-of-the-art Airboarding circuit, but that particular activity worried him. Speeding across the track and zipping through tight turns while hovering four inches off the ground sounded much too dangerous to both Zimmer and Bauer, but they conceded that it offered an alternative way to increase physical activity. The two scientists were more old-school and secretly hoped that soccer would hold the crew's interest. Now, in a few days, the star travelers would gather for their first soccer tournament of the voyage. Spirits were high in anticipation.

As the laughter subsided, Kylie Rickman pulled her knees up

to her chest and wrapped her arms around her legs. With a coy look she addressed her companions.

"You know, I've seen the trophy."

"No way," Gap said. "How?"

"You forget that Channy is my roommate. She's hiding it from everyone until the first champions are decided. But she's just dying to show someone—you know how she is about keeping a secret—and the other night she pulled it out and showed me."

"And?" Angelina said. "What does it look like?"

"Like I could tell you," Kylie said.

"Oh, c'mon," Angelina cried. "If Channy can't keep a secret, why should you?"

"Sorry," Kylie said. "I'm not telling. Not even if . . ." She paused, her eyes sparkling.

"Not even if what?" Angelina said, leaning forward.

Kylie's eyes widened and her mouth dropped open in mock terror. "Not even if you kicked me right in the head."

The group exploded in more laughter, and Angelina threw her napkin at Kylie, who ducked in time for it to fly over her. Both girls grinned at each other, enjoying the evening's fun.

Suddenly the red light over the Dining Hall's vidscreen began to flash, and a soft series of tones drifted out of the speakers. It signaled an announcement that would be broadcast throughout *Galahad*. A moment later Triana's face appeared on the screen.

"Hi, everyone," she began. Her expression was neutral, a look that most of the crew was used to by now. All ten sets of eyes in the Dining Hall were fixed on the screen, a scene that was being played out in every section of *Galahad*.

"Well, we're on our way," Tree said. "We all knew that there would be some tough times. We knew that eventually we would all have to pull together, to help us get through some difficult situations. I just don't think any of us thought we would be tested so soon.

"I planned on having a meeting with the entire crew after we were about three or four weeks out. I don't think a lot of meetings are necessary. You all know your jobs, you know what's expected of you, and I think it's better if you're left alone to do those jobs. But, given the circumstances of the last few days, I'm moving our first meeting up to tomorrow morning."

Gap and Kylie exchanged glances. It had all of the signs of an emergency meeting, but Tree refused to label it that way. Just "a meeting." Another sign that Dr. Zimmer knew what he was doing when he named Triana Martell to lead the mission.

"Those of you on duty tomorrow morning will obviously be unable to attend, but we will cover it on the vidscreens. I expect everyone else to join us at eight thirty in the Learning Center. It shouldn't take long. Thanks, and we'll see you in the morning."

With that, her image faded, leaving a dark gray screen. The group in the Dining Hall sat silent for a moment, then relaxed and looked around at each other. It was Mitchell who spoke first.

"Well, I'm working tomorrow morning. You guys have fun without me."

With a few exchanges of "good night" and "see you tomorrow," the group split up and trudged out of the room. Gap Lee was the last to leave, waving his hand across the sensor that slowly cut the lights and left the room in darkness.

Five minutes later the door to the Dining Hall opened, and a shadowy figure crept quietly inside.

18

The two men sat in front of the dark vidscreen. The newscast had just ended, and Dr. Zimmer had switched off the screen in disgust. Dr. Bauer looked at his boss.

"Do you want to talk about it?"

"There's not much to discuss," Dr. Zimmer said. "The man is crazy. He's crazy."

The man was Tyler Scofield. The news had just broadcast a report from a rally that Zimmer's old colleague had organized to protest the *Galahad* project. Now that the final 251 crew members had been announced Scofield was using the event to blast the mission and its director.

"Of course he'll get publicity for these rallies," Dr. Bauer said. "Look, there are pockets of discontent around the world, but his group is the only one that's united and actually taking action. The newshounds will always want to cover something that's contrary and extremist."

"He's stirring up way too much trouble," Zimmer said. "Did you hear the phrases he used? 'A dictator choosing his subjects?' 'Selection governed by ego?' 'Masses ignored in cowardly flight?' Cowardly! Because he insists that attention be focused on curing Bhaktul Disease rather than on saving what little of humanity we can." He shook his head, then pointed at the blank screen. "He's doing everything in his power to turn public opinion against our project, and to make this some sort of personal vendetta."

"People won't listen to him," Dr. Bauer said. "There's too much momentum with *Galahad*. We're less than two months from—"

His comment was interrupted by a severe cough, followed by another. He grabbed his chest and bent forward. Sweat broke out on his forehead. Dr. Zimmer reached out a hand and gently touched his assistant on the forearm.

"Can I get you something, Fenton?"

"No," Dr. Bauer said between heavy breaths. "It's nothing, really. I just get a spasm every now and then. It's already over. I'm fine."

Dr. Zimmer knew that was a lie, but he let the incident pass without further comment. Dr. Bauer had been seeing the best physicians in order to stave off the encroaching Bhaktul Disease. He was slowly losing the fight, but obviously insistent upon maintaining his pride. A few reports had claimed Bhaktul would often affect the mental capacities of its victims, driving some to insanity. Zimmer was sure that this was his colleague's biggest fear. Bauer's entire career was built on the foundation of his adept mind. He could handle the coughing; an attack on his brain, however, would be unthinkable.

"Anyway," Bauer said finally, "what I was saying was that we're less than two months from launch. There's not enough time for Scofield to rally enough people to stop us. He's just a news story right now."

"You might be right. But I still want to boost security. Nobody—absolutely nobody—gets inside this compound without clearance."

"Understood," Bauer said. "There's some good news, by the way."

"Please, anything!" Zimmer said.

"That report about the ship's construction falling behind? Well, not true. I spoke with the Space Authority about an hour ago and they say the first payload of equipment and supplies is ready to be loaded aboard. They'll launch the first sealed containers for the Storage Sections early next week."

"And you're sure you don't need my help with those?" Zimmer said.

Dr. Bauer shook his head. "No, I told you I would handle the Storage Sections. You've got enough on your hands. Let me take care of those."

He started to get up, then paused and looked across at the project director.

"Oh, and another thing. Roy Orzini wants to meet with us about that computer creation of his."

"What's up?"

Bauer shrugged. "Not sure. But I can guess. He wrote me a pretty stern e-mail yesterday."

"About?"

"About shifting more control of the ship from the kids to . . . to—what's it called now? Roc?"

Zimmer smiled. "And why is he unhappy about that? He tells me that Roc can handle anything."

"Yeah, that's what he tells me, too," Bauer said. "But I think he's starting to wonder if we're putting too many eggs in one basket."

"Meaning what? That we're putting too much control in Roc's hands, and that if there's a problem—"

"—then the ship will be in trouble," Bauer said. "Yeah, that's what he thinks."

"But you disagree."

Bauer sat still for a moment, thinking about his answer.

"Listen, it's not that these kids aren't very bright," he said. "On the contrary, we've picked the brightest of the bright. They're brilliant. But they're kids. We're putting so much pressure on them, so much weight on those teenage shoulders, that—in my opinion—anything we can do to lighten that load will be critical. So, yeah, I'm afraid I have to disagree with the very excitable Mr. Orzini. He tells us that Roc can handle it; then I say let the computer handle it all, and let these kids mature into the responsibilities over time."

Dr. Zimmer considered this for a minute.

"Well," he said, "you make a good point. Tell Roy we can talk tonight at dinner. I at least owe him the chance to make his case."

"Okay," Bauer said. "And speaking of dinner, if you need me this afternoon I'll be wrapping up the delivery of those seeds for *Galahad*'s farm. You'll be relieved to know that so far every country's shipments have been on time. Our little colonists are going to be eating quite well."

Dr. Zimmer took off his glasses and rubbed his forehead. "Well, delightful," he said with a touch of weariness in his voice. "But I won't truly feel relieved until these kids are gone. Away from Bhaktul. And away from Tyler Scofield."

T riana sat at the desk in her room, biting her lip and staring at the piles she had rearranged twice without doing anything to eliminate the clutter. She had scribbled a few notes on her electronic work pad for this morning's meeting, but had set it aside in favor of her personal journal.

The crew needs to be reassured that things are fine. We're on course, all systems are operating smoothly. But I can feel a sense of panic starting to creep in. Just saying everything's okay is a mistake. They won't buy that, and I don't blame them. Dad used to say "people will tolerate bad news; they won't tolerate deception. Shoot straight." So now I have to somehow break the news without spooking them even more.

She closed the journal and swapped her pen for the work pad stylus. It was time to get back to work, time to finish her speech to the crew. Looking at it now, she grimaced at all of the lines she had written and scratched out. Her communication skills were very good, but she was having a hard time deciding how to approach this. The stylus hung about half an inch above the work pad, waiting for some type of signal from her brain. Nothing was coming to her now, so she set it down.

"Roc," she called out. "What am I doing here?"

The mellow voice of Roy Orzini answered her. "Are you writing an essay called 'Why Roc Is the Coolest Thing in the Solar System and Beyond'?"

"I mean, what am I doing here? On this ship? In this position of . . . of . . ."

"Leadership?" Roc said.

"Well, yeah," Tree said. "Why did Sela have to back out? Why didn't they choose Gap as her replacement? Why not Bon, for that matter? He seems to know everything."

"He certainly seems to know how to push your hot buttons," Roc said. "Pardon me for saying this, Tree, but don't you think it's time you quit pouting?"

"Pouting?"

"You've been pouting since the day we left. First, you couldn't seem to leave fast enough, and now that we *have* left you're acting like you don't want to be here at all. You're pouting. And it's very unbecoming."

When Tree didn't respond, Roc continued. "You know, a lot of people thought that it took a long, long list of qualifications in order to be considered for this mission. There were a lot of people who never nominated their children or their students because they thought the odds were too tough. But the truth is, Dr. Zimmer really had just two main requirements. Would you like to know what they were?"

"Gap says we were picked for our brains and bravery," Triana said.

"Gap fell on his head a few too many times when he was a gymnast," Roc shot back. "That would be the simplest of answers, and maybe what someone else might have searched for. But not Dr. Z."

"So what was he looking for?"

"He would pull my plug if he knew I was telling you this. But I think you should know what made you pass the test. First, you had to be not just smart, but quick to absorb new ideas and new solutions. A genius with a closed mind is worthless on this trip. Worthless in general, some might say. I should know; I'm a genius."

Tree thought about that for a moment, biting her lip again. "And second?"

"Second, complete confidence in your own ability. Dr. Zimmer wanted young people who believed in themselves and believed that they were special. Not cocky, but confident."

Triana sat still, staring at her desk without seeing it. What Roc had said was true; every kid on *Galahad* was sure they belonged on the mission. She believed it, too. This was her place, her time, her calling. This was what she was born to.

So why the doubts now? Why the confusion? Was this one of the defining moments of her command? Of her life? And was she up to the challenge?

Roc broke the silence. "Your father knew that you should be here."

Tree looked up with a start. "What are you talking about? My dad didn't even know I was selected—"

"That's right," Roc said. "He died before the selection process was finished. But he knew you were a candidate."

"How do you know this?"

"Because he sent a personal data disc directly to Dr. Zimmer and the *Galahad* committee. It was all about you. Your courage. Your loyalty. Your intellect. It was one of the last things he did before going to the hospital."

Triana's eyes started to fill with tears, but she let Roc continue.

"Your father had no idea what the criteria for selection were. But he knew his daughter, and knew what was inside you. When he and your mother separated, you spent time with both parents, but made your own decision to live with your father. Your mother consented without argument.

"When faced with choices in education, you didn't hesitate. You chose the most demanding classes in the most demanding school. You knew you would succeed, and you did.

"When your father fell ill, you chose to sacrifice your sports, your hobbies, and your free time to attend to him. Other families requested special assistance; you believed you could handle the responsibility, and you did.

"So you're going through yet another difficult time," Roc added. "I don't believe anyone else on *Galahad* is better equipped to handle it than you. Dr. Zimmer felt the same way. And so did your father."

Triana remained still and quiet. One solitary tear had started to make its way down her cheek, but it never had a chance. She wiped it away and picked up the stylus pen from her desk.

Bending over and resting her head on one hand, she began writing again on her work pad. After a silent minute of concentration she said, "Thank you, Roc."

"You're welcome. Now back to work. And remember, it's not just 'coolest in the solar system,' it's 'coolest in the solar system and beyond.'"

20

There were two weeks left before the crew of *Galahad* would leave their home planet and enter the Incubator orbiting as part of the space station. Their training was about as complete as could be expected. As Dr. Armistead put it, "We could work with them for another two years and still not prepare them for everything they're going to encounter."

Wallace Zimmer didn't want their last two weeks on Earth spent in training. Instead he sent each of them home. He gathered them all together for a final briefing before they scattered. "Soak up everything you possibly can," he said. "If you love the beach, spend hours and hours on the beach. If you love the mountains, climb every one you can. If you want to walk in the forest, inhale every fresh breath of pine that you can. Come back with your sensory organs overloaded. Stock up enough memories to last you five years.

"And one other thing," he added as he watched their eyes begin to mist over. "Embrace your loved ones. Tell them everything you've ever wanted to say to them. Show them how much you love them." He tapped his chest softly. "Let them know that you will carry them with you on your journey, that they will never be far away. Comfort them, and let them comfort you."

He looked out among the many faces, the faces from dozens

of countries, each representing a unique history and outlook. The faces of Eos, staring back at him, making him proud.

"I want to tell you to have fun," he said, "but I don't expect you to. Good-byes are never easy. I suspect that most of you will grow up more in the next two weeks than at any other point in your lives."

With a few closing instructions from Dr. Armistead regarding their return and what items they could and could not bring, the group stood up slowly and filed out of the room. Triana lingered behind, which was not surprising to Dr. Zimmer. He waited until the room had emptied before he came to sit next to her.

"Dr. Armistead tells me that you're staying here for these two weeks," he said softly. "Is that right?"

Triana fidgeted in her seat for a moment, biting her lip. "Yes," she said. "I don't really have anywhere to go."

"You still have no interest in seeing your mother? We can fly you out to Indianapolis this afternoon."

Triana shook her head. "No, thanks."

"What about Colorado? It might do you good to see some old friends and do a little hiking in the hills."

"No, but thank you. I don't . . ." She paused for a second. "My memories of that stuff are with my dad. I think that's how I'd like to leave them."

Zimmer took a long, deep breath. "Tree, you have become very special to me over the last year and a half. It sounds very corny to say, I know, but you are the closest thing to a daughter that I've known in my life. When you have excelled in your studies, I've been proud. When you've struggled with the responsibilities that come with leadership, I've secretly cheered you on." He put his arm around her. "And when you hurt, I hurt a little bit, too."

When she spoke, her voice was barely above a whisper. "I'm ready to launch right now," she said. "The only person I needed to say good-bye to was my dad, and they wouldn't let me do that."

"I understand," Dr. Zimmer said. "It's your decision, of

course. I won't tell you how to spend your time before you head up to the Incubator. But I'd like to give you something to think about for the next two weeks, if that's okay."

She sat quietly, staring ahead, so he continued. "Every person deals with grief in their own unique way. Some people break down into intense crying fits. Others cling to their friends and family, leaning on them for support. I think the fact that you're angry about it is fine, Tree. You have a right to be angry. The closest person to you in the world was taken away, and the rest of your world is being turned upside down at the same time. I don't blame you for wanting to run away. *Galahad* is your getaway vehicle, in a sense.

"But I think you'll discover something for yourself before too long. You can't ever run away from your pain. It's like your shadow, Tree. It will drag along behind you no matter how far you run. Leaving Earth will not magically disconnect your feelings and your anger about your dad. When you arrive at Eos you'll feel the same sense of loss that you feel today."

She was still quiet, but he could tell that she was listening, absorbing what he was saying. That was one of her qualities that he appreciated the most. Triana never seemed to make snap judgments without weighing all of the information. Her decisions were firm, but at least they were well considered.

"You'll have a lot of people on this ship who would love nothing more than to be friends with you," he said. "If you give them a chance I think you'll find that they can help you. Not just with the duties of running the mission, but with your life, too."

Triana nodded slowly. "Okay," was all she said.

He patted her on the shoulder, then stood up. "And in the meantime," he said, "please don't be so anxious to leave everything behind. A day will come when you'll wish you had these two weeks back again."

He smiled at her, then turned and walked out of the room. She sat alone, biting her lip and drumming her fingers on her knee.

21

By eight fifteen, the Learning Center, or simply School, as it was usually called, was buzzing. Essentially an auditorium, it had 250 seats curved in a half circle facing the stage. Rows of stadium seats ascended high enough to provide everyone a good view. *Galahad's* ongoing educational courses would take place here, with Roc providing the lesson plans and tutorials. A giant vidscreen hung behind the stage, a window into the giant warehouse of knowledge stored within the ship.

The room was also the natural meeting place whenever an assembly of the crew was required. This morning, of the 251 crew members, forty-five were obliged to be on duty, carrying out the tasks necessary to keep the ship running smoothly. The majority of those were at the Farms, tending to the fragile resources that provided a hungry crew with nourishment for the long voyage. Others were handling the maintenance chores that kept *Galahad* clean and in top condition.

The remainder of the crew, however, were finding a seat for this first meeting called by Triana. A smattering of nervous laughter could be heard while greetings and waves were exchanged. One by one the Council members walked in and quickly made their way to the front of the auditorium.

Triana stepped inside at precisely eight thirty. *Galahad's* video cameras picked her up as she stepped to the podium, her image and voice ready to be transmitted to the ship's monitors and the working crew who couldn't attend.

The large group facing her quieted down as she peered first at her notes on the work pad before her, then at the assembled crew.

"Thank you for being here on time," she began. "I promise to have you out of here before nine o'clock, because as you probably know by now, I'm not very gabby."

A ripple of laughter spread across the room. Lita, who was sitting in the front row with the other Council members, gave her friend a look of encouragement.

Triana cleared her throat and continued. "Let me first say that you've all done remarkably well during this first week. All of the work has been finished on schedule, all of the departments are in perfect shape, and no one has been hurt. Well . . ." she cracked a faint smile. "Not counting three Boarding injuries. Lita says two were just bruises and scrapes, one was a broken finger. Thank you for at least wearing your helmets."

"With these three guys, helmets wouldn't matter!" Channy yelled from the first row. "There's not much bouncing around in those thick skulls to get damaged."

More laughter from the group, with several people hissing and pointing at the three daredevils in the crowd.

When the auditorium began to quiet again, Triana's look turned serious.

"But there's no use acting like everything is normal. We all know about the encounter that Peter reported."

Most of the crew members recognized that the word "encounter" was a respectful way to acknowledge the incident, and a thoughtful gesture to Peter, who was sitting somewhere among the sea of faces.

"I also sent a mass e-mail regarding an historical coin that Gap found down by the Storage Sections," Tree continued. "No one has replied, so I'm assuming it does not belong to any crew member."

The room was now deadly silent, with only the faint breath of the ventilators recharging the air.

"And you all know about the crude graffiti. All of this has made our first week uneasy. The worst part is that we don't know who is responsible for any of this."

In the auditorium a few heads nodded slowly, but no one made a sound. Tree glanced down at the Council in the front row, then back up at the anxious crew members staring at her.

"While we don't know anything concrete right now, I can tell you this much. Roc has finished gathering data from our ship records and performed a few calculations based on some new information from Lita. He's informed me that the ship's energy readings are slightly out of whack. Since then he's eliminated a couple of possibilities, and right now believes strongly that the most likely explanation"—Tree paused ever so slightly—"is an additional person somewhere on _Galahad_."

She expected a rush of noise, the sound of two hundred people exclaiming surprise and alarm. But the room remained eerily quiet. Had they all been so sure of this announcement that the meeting itself was anticlimactic? Or were they frozen with fear?

Looking at their faces individually, she realized her mistake. They were not paralyzed by fear; they were simply waiting for her to lead. They trusted her judgment and valued her leadership skills. The crew of _Galahad_ was on the alert, awaiting instructions from their general. She was immediately awash with a sense of pride.

Triana placed both hands on the podium. "I will be meeting with the rest of the Council to discuss security procedures. Obviously this is not something that we—or Dr. Zimmer—ever planned on. But every one of you will be kept fully informed of each move we make. We don't conduct secret operations on this ship. Our job on the Council is to lead, but your input and suggestions will be welcome at any time. Are there any questions?"

A few hands went up. One girl asked about leaving the lights on daylight mode at all times. No, this would not happen yet.

Another girl wanted to know if Roc had any thoughts about who the intruder could be? One of the workers who helped build *Galahad,* maybe? It would be useless to guess at this point, Tree told her.

A boy in the back of the room raised his hand and asked if there was a chance they might turn back for Earth.

"No," Tree said firmly. "It would take weeks to reorient the ship for a trip back to Earth. Then who knows how long it might take to launch again. We could lose as much as a year or two. That's not an option.

"Besides," she said, her voice growing even stronger. "We will not rely on Earth to fix our problems. We can't run home to Mommy every time something comes up. We'd better get used to the fact that we are responsible for ourselves. If someone wants to mess with us, they obviously don't know who they're dealing with."

There was a moment's pause, then the sound of three or four people clapping. In seconds the entire room was engulfed with the applause. The crew of *Galahad* was on its feet, clapping and whistling, ready to take on the enemy. Ready for Triana to lead them.

In the front row, Lita cheered. *Galahad* might be in trouble. But it was in good hands.

22

With five weeks to go before the launch Dr. Zimmer had arrived at the space station with Dr. Bauer. Dr. Armistead had remained behind to wrap up any last details at the training complex and to escort the crew when it was their time to leave. In another eight days they would all be brought into space and housed inside the Incubator for the final month.

Zimmer was anxious about some last-minute changes that had become necessary on *Galahad*. Construction had proceeded at lightning speed, and for the most part it would be ready to go when the time came.

The agricultural domes were finished and already sported some crops basking in the artificial sunlight. Seeds and plants from around the world continued to arrive daily. A few of the insects that had been approved for the trip—bees to assist pollination and earthworms to help aerate the soil and produce fertilizer—were hard at work and apparently content in their new home.

The Storage Sections were filling up and almost ready to be sealed. Dr. Bauer was primarily in charge of this department, and had agreed with Dr. Zimmer that keeping them locked until the crew reached Eos was crucial. "Don't even give them the chance to ransack the supplies that they'll need when they arrive," Bauer had said. "It's easy to say now that they'll stay out on their own, but who knows what will be going through their minds after a year or two in isolation. Not even these kids are perfect." With a scowl he added, "Believe me, no kids are." Zimmer found it hard to believe that the crew would ransack anything, but nodded agreement.

The crew's apartments were also finished, sitting vacant and awaiting their personal finishing touches. All of the water recycling plants were functioning, the air recycling system was in good shape, and Roc was already skimming through checklist after checklist to make certain that the launch would be successful.

Yet Zimmer wasn't naïve enough to think that everything would be perfect. And it wasn't.

"Tell me again why we only have eight Spiders, and not ten," he said to the tall, thin man sitting across from his desk.

"Listen, I can put all ten of them on board," the design engineer said, "but I'm telling you that only eight of them will work."

His name was Sun Koyama. For almost two years his team had worked day and night, designing, building and assembling the largest craft ever conceived. He was exhausted, mentally and physically, and was in no mood to be lectured by anyone.

"Where was the slipup?" Zimmer said.

"This is not a slipup. I told Dr. Bauer months ago that the company responsible for the internal fittings on the Spiders was in trouble. Their workforce is dwindling, people are dropping out with Bhaktul or just quitting to be with their families, and the same thing is happening with their suppliers. They put all of their remaining staff to work and have eight Spiders finished. The other two are just empty shells. If you ask me, we should be grateful we got eight."

Zimmer sighed. Koyama was right, of course. It was a miracle that work on *Galahad* had gone as smoothly as it had. Companies around the world were shutting down as their employees became ill, and motivation was a problem. After all, it wasn't their children who were being placed aboard the spacecraft. Many were starting to ask, "Why am I doing this?"

Now *Galahad* would launch with two fewer escape crafts than originally planned. The egg-shaped vehicles were to serve several purposes. For one thing they could be used to maneuver outside the spaceship in case any repairs were necessary. They were fitted with multiple arms, some designed to lift large, bulky objects, and others specially made for smaller precision work. With the arms extended they almost resembled an insect, and it wasn't long before they were simply called Spiders.

They were also the vehicles that would transport the crew to the surface when *Galahad* reached its destination. Each Spider was built to accommodate up to thirty passengers, so losing two meant that arrangements would have to be made. Dr. Zimmer scribbled a few notes on his workpad and looked at his calendar. Launch was scheduled in thirty-eight days.

"All right," he said to Koyama. "I want to go ahead and load all ten of them. These last two can still fly, right?"

"Yes, they'll fly," the engineer said. "But they can't support life inside."

"Well, who knows, the kids might need them for spare parts, or something," Zimmer said. "No sense leaving them docked here at the station."

Koyama grunted a reply and left. His job was nearly finished and he was ready to go home.

Alone in his office, Zimmer coughed loudly and noticed the taste of blood.

23

O f all the stuff I've got crammed inside my chips, let me tell you something I'm glad I don't have: hormones.

I'm very familiar with the human need for acceptance and friendship and companionship. But this whole "love" thing has me a little baffled. I've read everything I can find about it, I've asked Roy—that was a big mistake—and I've even tried listening to some of the most popular love songs. Thank goodness computers can't hurl. Humans are such a tortured bunch, aren't they?

And from some of the eavesdropping I've done, I will be completely amazed if we throw 251 teenagers into a spaceship and go five years without some drama.

Two dozen crew members were scattered at tables around the Dining Hall. They had begun streaming in as the lights gently came up, and now, at seven o'clock, breakfast was under way. The sound of muted conversation mingled with the scrapes and clinks of glasses and silverware. Every few seconds another cluster of teens would walk in, either wiping the remnants of sleep out of their eyes, or glowing with the effects of a morning workout.

Channy scurried in behind Lita and tapped her on the shoulder. Lita, just reaching for a tray, turned and smiled.

"Wow, I can't believe how quickly you can get here after leading the morning workout. I could never get ready that fast."

"You should chop off your hair like me," Channy said. "Now I can be ready almost as fast as a boy." She picked up her own tray and fixed Lita with a hard look. "Speaking of workouts—"

"Yes, I know," Lita said. "I wasn't being lazy, though. I was actually at work."

"Someone sick?"

"No. Sick House is empty this morning. I was just checking a few things for Roc."

Channy picked up an energy block, then changed her mind and exchanged it with another. "I need to get out of this rut," she explained to Lita. "I can't have raspberry *every* morning. Today I'm definitely apple."

"You're a rebel."

"So, what's up with Roc? He can't do his own work, or what?"

Lita filled a glass with simulated orange juice. "No, we just used the, uh, incident with Peter Meyer to check our energy levels. It's possible that excess stress might throw the levels out of whack compared to normal readings. Multiply that times two hundred fifty people and it might make a big difference."

"And?"

"It didn't, really. At least not any more than we thought. I fed the new info to Roc just a few minutes ago."

The two girls found a table and sat down.

"I thought Roc had already decided it was the stowaway who was throwing off the readings," Channy said. "What does he want with this new information?"

"I'm not sure, but I think he's trying to . . . I don't know, maybe identify the person."

Channy raised her eyebrows. "What? You mean use the energy readings like a fingerprint or something?"

"Yeah," Lita said, "something like that. Or at least narrow it down to where he can say it's a forty-year-old man or sixty-five-year-old." She took a bite of her energy block and looked across the table at her fellow Council member.

"You know, Channy, he's the same ol' Roc every time. And I know this sounds stupid, because he *is* a machine, after all, but . . ."

She paused. Channy kept quiet, silently chewing her food.

"But somehow I get a weird feeling from him, like he's . . . I don't know . . . worried, maybe?" She brushed her lips with a napkin. "As I said, I know it sounds stupid."

Channy swallowed some juice, then wiped her mouth. "Oh, I don't know. Roy put an awful lot of himself into that machine. I don't see why some of his real personality couldn't have leaked into it."

"Now you're sounding as silly as I am," Lita said with a laugh. "Listen, forget I even said anything. I was probably just tired. He got me up and into Sick House at five o'clock."

"Hmm. You should have been working out."

"Hey, I'll hit one of the afternoon groups. They're usually more fun anyway."

"Cuter guys, too," Channy said, grinning. "I know one in particular who probably wishes you would take an afternoon session permanently."

"Oh, here we go." Lita shook her head. "Your Cupid outfit is showing again."

"Hey, I think I'm pretty good at matching people up," Channy said. "Believe me, I see people at their best and their worst. Mixing and matching is easy when you see both sides. The only person I can't figure out is Tree. She's a mystery. I have *no* idea who might be perfect for her."

Lita ate her breakfast thoughtfully. "Well, she might be quiet and tough-acting, but she's still a girl. It's not like she doesn't have a heart."

Channy had her juice halfway to her mouth and stopped, slowly putting it back down on the table. "Wait a minute," she said. "Why didn't I think of that? You're probably closer to her than anyone else. Are you holding out on me?"

"What are you talking about?"

"C'mon, girl. If you know something about the Ice Queen, then spill."

Lita laughed out loud. "Channy, you crack me up. First of all, if I *did* know something, I probably would just send everyone an e-mail. It's a faster way to spread information to the whole crew than telling you. Not *much* faster, but a little."

Channy stuck her tongue out playfully.

"But," Lita said, "that 'Ice Queen' label isn't fair, either. I told you, Triana has a heart. She might not show it, but she can have feelings for someone. I think she does, in fact."

"Well?" Channy leaned forward. "Out with it."

"No, Channy. Look, I don't know for sure. It's just a hunch, really. A few things here and there that she's let drop about someone. I think she's attracted to him, but she's too wrapped up with the mission to take a step."

Picking up her tray, Channy stood and downed the last of her juice. "Well, if she's got the hots for someone, I'll figure it out." She narrowed her eyes playfully. "I always do."

Lita laughed again and rose to her feet. "I should have known better than to say anything to you."

Channy started toward the door, calling back over her shoulder. "Hold out on me, Lita, and I'll work you out this afternoon until you're down on one knee."

Smiling, Lita followed her out the door, and two other kids moved into the spot they had vacated. Sitting at the next table, with his back to them, Gap Lee sat quietly, digesting not his breakfast, which sat untouched, but what he had just overheard.

Not even his early morning run had caused his heart to race like it was right now.

24

"T his is not a pleasure cruise."

Dr. Wallace Zimmer had said this so many times during their training that it became a running joke with the crew. Whenever it seemed as if the young would-be space explorers were losing their focus, the scientist would sigh heavily and explain—again—the importance of being prepared.

"You can't come back for follow-up training, you know," he would preach. "If you think this is just some pleasure cruise or a quick vacation, you're wrong."

The five Council members took his message to heart, and even decided to have a little fun with him. He had scheduled a final meeting with them, the day before they entered the Incubator. It would be their last visit with anyone outside of their group. Zimmer had dreaded this moment for a long time. These star travelers had become the children he had never had. Too busy with his career and studies to pursue a serious relationship, he had never married. He was close to fifty before he looked up from his work to realize that a lifetime of educational opportunities had prevented him from exploring a life with another person.

The time he had spent with *Galahad*'s crew had filled that vacancy in his life.

He entered the room, notes in hand, ready to swallow his

deep personal sorrow and maintain a strong, professional image for the teens. He stopped short in the doorway, his mouth falling open. Then he dropped his notes to the floor.

All five members of the Council were standing there, decked out in beach clothes: swimsuits, sunglasses, Hawaiian shirts and more. Gap and Channy had life preservers hanging from their necks, and even the ever-serious Bon had a straw hat on his head.

Channy stepped forward, took the gray-haired man by the hand and told him, "We're ready for our pleasure cruise, Dr. Zimmer."

With that, he broke down. After devoting almost three years of his life to *Galahad* and its young crew, his work was over. He cried, the tears beginning slowly, and then escalating into uncontrollable sobs. Channy brought him over to a chair, and the Council gathered around, some sitting on the floor by his feet, the others in chairs next to him. Soon everyone was either crying or fighting back tears. The realization that this was good-bye was overwhelming.

Wallace Zimmer decided to cry himself out. There was nothing for which he needed to save his tears. The disease from Comet Bhaktul had begun settling in him, and although he hid the symptoms from the crew members, he knew that it would not be long before he was bedridden. He calculated that he would be gone before *Galahad* was beyond Neptune. These kids were the closest people in his life, and when they left he fully believed that his will to live would be leaving with them. The beginning of their mission would mark the end of his.

For almost five minutes he wept. The Council members were patient, willing to devote any amount of time to this father figure. Finally, he looked into the eyes of each of them and managed to say, "Are you ready?"

Triana nodded. "You've *made* us ready, Dr. Z."

He smiled at her, and put out his hand. Gap had picked up the scientist's notes from the floor and now handed them to him.

"Will Dr. Armistead or Dr. Bauer be joining us?" Channy said.

The scientist shook his head sadly. "I'm sorry. Dr. Bauer requested that he spend his last few weeks with his family. He told me to apologize for not personally seeing you off. I think the disease has affected him to the point where he was embarrassed to have you see him. He didn't want that to be your last memory of him. I gave him permission to leave on the shuttle for Earth last night. He should be home by this time tomorrow."

The room grew quiet as the impact of Bhaktul struck them once again. The Council members had never been as close to Bauer as they were to Dr. Zimmer, but he had been a vital teammate nonetheless.

Zimmer said, "And Dr. Armistead will say her good-byes when she packs you into the Incubator. She's pretty broken up right now." More silence gripped the room. Now, not only was the impact of the disease hitting home, but so was the realization that they would soon be saying good-bye to everyone they knew on Earth.

For the next two hours they talked about every aspect of their mission. The responsibilities of the Council. The necessity of maintaining order and discipline for the entire five years. How the Storage Sections in the lower levels would remain sealed and off-limits until reaching Eos.

And the cycles of work.

Roc was the brain of *Galahad,* but the crew was the muscle. Each member was expected to shoulder their share of duties each week in a department overseen by one of the Council members. Groups of thirty or thirty-one would spend six weeks in one department, then rotate randomly into another department for another six-week assignment. After three or four such tours a crew member would be granted a six-week leave, so at any given time sixty people would be on a sort of vacation. Then it was back into the rotation to work in the other departments.

The Council members were the only ones exempt from the

rotation. For their three-year term they would remain with their department. Once a new Council was elected, the original group would fall into the same rotation as the rest of the crew.

Dr. Zimmer appreciated the fact that some of his young explorers were especially skilled in one area, such as medicine or engineering. Yet he was insistent that everyone learn from each department. When *Galahad* reached Eos it would need all 251 colonists to share as much knowledge as possible to tame a new world. Should something tragic happen to some of the crew members, he didn't want their expertise to vanish with them.

And on a mission like this, anything could happen.

Education was another matter. *Galahad* was not only a lifeboat, but a traveling university as well. Each crew member would continue their education during the journey. The ship's computer banks were crammed with every bit of information the mission planners could think to send with them: math, science, biology, astronomy, medicine and history. Great works of literature were stored as well, along with manuals and blueprints for building a new civilization on an alien world.

Biographies of Earth's most influential people were loaded aboard, including philosophers, scholars, poets, leaders and civil rights pioneers.

Every crew member would pore through the material. It was predicted that when *Galahad* pulled into orbit around its new star home, it would contain 251 college graduates, each of who would hold the equivalent of four degrees. Mankind's hope for the future would not be ill prepared for the challenge.

As their final meeting wrapped up, Dr. Zimmer stressed two critical points.

"You'll be working hard and studying much of the time," he told his first Council. "Please remember to make time for fun. Soccer, boarding, theater . . . I hope you put energy into these pursuits as well.

"And finally," he said, turning his head slowly to look at each of their faces. "Please look after each other. Be sensitive to each person's heart and mind. No two of you are exactly alike. That is by design. I wanted to challenge each and every one of you to expand your range of intellect and emotion. Learn from one another as you learn *about* one another. Learn to appreciate the skills your neighbor has that you may lack. Learn to take pride in the skills that are unique to you. Learn to respect one another.

"Remember that as of tomorrow, you have only one another to lean on."

He stood, and his handpicked Council joined him. Circling him, the group embraced quietly for more than a minute. Finally they heard Dr. Zimmer say softly, "I love you all."

He broke free, and without looking back walked out of the room.

25

B on Hartsfield was kneeling in the dirt, one large hand slowly scratching the soil. The scowl that usually etched his face was absent at the moment, replaced by a look of curiosity. As the Council member responsible for the Agricultural Department, he was happiest when he was at work in *Galahad*'s crops. Behind him stood Gap Lee, hands on his hips.

"Don't ignore the question, Bon."

"I'm not ignoring anything. But I have work to do, you know. I assume you *do* want to eat on this trip."

Gap walked around the kneeling figure so he could face Bon.

"I'm not trying to interrupt your work. Just answer the question. Are you really *that* upset with every single decision Triana makes, or is it mostly just an act? You know, the 'Bon the Bad Boy' image."

Bon tossed a small handful of dirt aside and wiped both hands on his pants. The two of them were not alone in *Galahad*'s farming section, but they were out of earshot from the other workers scattered among the rows of crops. Bright panels in the ceiling that mimicked sunlight cast a shower of light, preserving a tropical temperature around the clock. In order to look up at his fellow Council member, Bon had to shade his eyes with one hand.

"That's ridiculous," he said. "I don't have time for games. And I don't think I've spoken out against everything Triana has done. Just because I'm the most vocal when it comes to disagreeing does not make me a bad boy, either. *Someone* needs to speak up when something is wrong."

"Sure, I agree with that. But couldn't you be just a bit more team-oriented? Do all of your comments and suggestions have to sound so . . . aggressive?"

Bon chuckled. "I don't know how you were raised, Gap, but in Sweden I was brought up to say what I thought. This ship is in a little trouble right now, and I'm sorry if peoples' feelings aren't my first priority."

"Don't give me that," Gap said. "You act like you have to drive home every point with a sledgehammer. It's a little exhausting after a while." He glanced over at two crew members who were pulling a cart through the fields. The boy and the girl were laughing at something, and stopped now and then to readjust their grips on the cart.

Gap looked back at Bon. "All I'm saying is that you might try a little more diplomacy. Like explaining your opinions instead of trying to force them down Tree's throat."

Bon began to work the soil again, picking up a small dirt clod and breaking it apart. He waved away a bee that hovered around his face. Slowly his infamous scowl returned.

"All right," he said. "Now, let me give *you* a little advice. Quit trying to play politics all the time on the Council and open your eyes."

"And what does that mean?"

"It means you seem more interested in the title of Council member than the responsibilities. This little visit is a prime example. Aren't there more important things for you to be doing right now than chatting with me about Triana's feelings?"

Gap's face tightened into a grimace. He and Bon had become good friends during the first several months of their training, even though Bon was not an easy person to like. But Gap respected his strong work ethic and no-nonsense attitude. Over the last year, however, their friendship had become strained. Gap soon realized that this no-nonsense approach could become old very fast. Bon never seemed to lighten up, and for Gap, who was always quick with a joke to break the ice during their intense training, it seemed pointless.

The fact that Bon seemed to despise Triana was the final straw for Gap. He opened his mouth to respond to Bon's criticism, but was interrupted by a shout. It came from the two crew members who had been pulling the cart through the field.

Bon stood up and shouted back to them. "What is it?"

Instead of replying, the boy and the girl waved for Bon and Gap to join them quickly, and then knelt down as if examining something. Both Council members began to run through the rows of dirt and plants. As soon as they were within twenty feet of the kneeling figures they saw it.

A large section of the crop lay damaged. Dozens of plant stalks were broken into pieces and strewn across the ground. Others had been completely uprooted and cast aside. The ground had been churned up, as if someone had gouged into the soil with their feet.

Gap quickly scanned the area, looking for footprints leaving the scene. He finally spotted a set of tracks weaving out of the destruction zone and leading towards the exit.

Bon stood over the mess, seething. He looked back and forth, surveying the damage, and then looked up at Gap. The two boys exchanged a steely glance, breathing heavily. Words weren't necessary.

The intruder had left another calling card.

At the same moment, Triana was hunched over her work pad in the Conference Room. Channy and Lita sat on either side of her. The three girls had been working together for almost an hour, engaging Roc with questions, and then tossing ideas back and forth regarding the ship's crisis. Roc had patiently volunteered all the information he could.

Channy looked down at Triana's notes and said, "Okay, that pretty much settles it, right? This stowaway must be getting into the Storage Sections somehow. He couldn't be holed up anywhere else without being spotted."

"That's probably right," Lita said. "But how is he able to get in and out? These storage compartments are sealed. *We* don't even have access to them. I say we get a couple dozen people together and break in. There's no way he could fight off that many people."

Triana shook her head. "We don't have any idea if this person has weapons with him. I'm not taking a chance on him killing several crew members before we can jump him. So far all he's done is scare people and cause some vandalism. That's not worth getting someone killed."

"Well," Channy said, "what about trapping him inside? If we station enough people around all of the storage exits, he couldn't get in or out."

Tree considered this for a moment. "A siege," she finally said. "He would have to come out eventually for food and water. Unless . . ." Her voice trailed off.

"Unless what?" Channy said.

"Roc," Tree said, "I know you won't tell us what's in those sealed sections."

"You know, I had this same discussion with Gap," Roc said, "and not once have any of you offered me a good bribe. I can be bought. Try it."

Tree ignored this. "Can you at least tell us whether an intruder would have access to food and water inside those sections? If we bottled him up, would he be able to survive in there for a long time?"

Roc didn't answer right away. His analytical mind was racing, gauging whether divulging this bit of information would
violate his programming. Tree, Lita and Channy waited.

Finally Roc reached a decision. "If a person was able to get
inside those sections," he said slowly, "he would be able to sustain himself for quite a while." The three girls looked crest-
fallen.

"However," the computer added, "there is one other thing I
can tell you. In order to access those supplies, a person would
have to be intimately acquainted with this project."

"What do you mean?" Lita said.

"I mean that if our intruder was simply a project worker or a
staff member of the space station, he wouldn't know where to
find these supplies or how to retrieve them. Only someone close
to the *Galahad* project would have that information."

Tree bit her lip and thought about this for a moment. "So, if
we trapped this person inside, we wouldn't know if they were
stealing the supplies or not."

"Correct," Roc said. "And, I might add, there are two other
points to consider. One, *Galahad*'s crew is not trained for this
type of activity. Obviously no one expected you to be fighting
off an intruder within our own walls. Ninjas, you're not. Second, this crew is already stretched thin with work assignments. If you try to keep a sizable force stationed around the
Storage Sections—and that's a lot of room to cover—then
you're going to cripple the normal work production needed to
maintain the ship. And I'm not washing dishes, that's for
sure."

Triana dropped her stylus pen down on the work pad and
began rubbing her temple with one hand. She looked at Lita,
then Channy.

"We won't break in," she told them, "and we won't set up
camps outside the Storage Sections. At least not yet. Whoever
this intruder is, he's human, and that means he's bound to make

a mistake sometime. Every time he ventures out of his hole he's taking another chance that we catch him."

Lita put her hand on Tree's arm and raised her eyebrows. "Which brings up another question, doesn't it? Just what do we do when we catch him?"

26

The sun was just beginning to peek over the horizon. Since that horizon was made up of the Gulf of Mexico, the huge ball of fire would spread out across the waves, making the water dance with blinding yellow streaks. A small crescent moon was holding on to its last glint of light before the dawn washed it away.

Maria Marques sat with her bare feet in the sand, just beyond the reach of the encroaching waves as they splashed desperately upon the shore. Pieces of wood, seaweed and assorted marine life that had washed up overnight lay scattered around her like a child's toys at the end of the day. She watched the reflection of the sun, hardly moving a muscle, and seemed oblivious to the sounds of the town of Veracruz, Mexico, coming to life behind her.

It was almost six o'clock. Her husband still lay sleeping in their comfortable home about eight blocks away. Maria loved to come to the beach alone, and especially loved to catch a sunrise before making her way down the empty streets to her small medical office. The alone time was precious to her, affording her a chance to think without the noise of a busy household. Three children, a husband, her own mother, along with two dogs and two cats, all added up to a zoo. A loud zoo.

This was her escape.

Over the past two months it had been more than that. Since her oldest daughter had been selected for a spot on *Galahad*, Maria needed this time even more. She needed to summon all of her inner strength to be able to say good-bye soon.

Her daughter Lita was fourteen. When the time came to lock herself up in the enormous spacecraft she would be fifteen. And on her own.

Maria scooped a handful of sand and let it slowly seep between her fingers without taking her eyes off the water. When the sand ran out she grabbed another handful. Again and again she felt the cool, smooth grains run through her fingers. Her mind drifted, catching on glimpses of Lita at various stages of her young life.

Dressed only in her diaper, running through her father's grocery store, stretching out her hands to whatever she could reach on the shelves. Maria had run after her, laughing, trying to put the scattered items back in their proper places.

Lita's first day of school, practically clawing her way out of Maria's tearful grasp, anxious to get inside. Unlike the other children who cried and clutched at their parents' legs, Lita knew there were more books inside the school, and she couldn't wait to reach them.

At age twelve, setting aside her studies of Spanish explorers to help care for her younger brother and sister. Reading to them, mostly, her eyes wide with excitement as she weaved tales of De Soto, Pizarro, Cortez and Coronado. She would try, unsuccessfully, to enthrall her younger siblings with details of Cabeza de Vaca and Balboa, explorers who faced terrible hardships during their travels throughout Central and South America. "Many of these men made terrible mistakes," she would say to her little brother. "Some inflicted horrible treatment upon the native people they encountered. We all need to learn from their successes and their failures." Her brother would smile up at her, not really hearing what she was saying, just enjoying the attention he was receiving from his older sister. Maria would hear Lita sigh, and continue with her storytelling.

Two loud birds soared just over Maria's head as she sat on the beach, coming to rest at the water's edge. Their cries cut through the sound of the rushing waves, cries of sadness it seemed. Maria grasped another handful of sand and began to drift again. Remembering the mixture of excitement and sadness when Lita was selected from thousands of nominees for the *Galahad* mission. Lita's mouth had opened into a round, soundless *O*, not sure how to respond in front of her grieving mother and father.

Maria had wondered how she would tell her other children that their older sister was leaving, permanently. In the end, she needn't have worried, because it was Lita who took them aside and gently explained. Lita, who would be following in the footsteps of so many Spanish explorers, taking a path that her ancestors could never have imagined. A pathway to the stars.

That journey would begin in just a few hours. Maria looked up and managed to catch one or two specks of starlight, quickly dissipating as the sun began to break the horizon.

Releasing a last handful of sand, she rose to her feet, turned her back on the sunrise, and walked home.

27

hree days had passed with no further signs from the mysterious guest aboard *Galahad*. The crew went about their business, trying to maintain a normal pace and attitude. They did their jobs, ate their meals, socialized and exercised. But they did it with their eyes wide open, and too many cautious glances over their shoulders. The air was uncomfortable.

It was a topic that Triana felt she should address one evening as she rode the stationary bike in the exercise room. Lita was puffing along beside her as video images of a winding mountain road flashed on the wall before them.

"We're a frightened ship, and I don't like that," Triana said. "The intruder is doing exactly what he wants to do: making us nervous and jumpy."

"His tactics are obvious," Lita said. "The damage to the crops wasn't extensive, just enough to aggravate us. So he wasn't trying to wreck our food supply. He just wanted us to know that he could."

She paused to catch her breath, sweat dripping off her forehead. Then she added, "And psychologically that's worse. I think his primary goal is to get us frightened and angry. He's hoping the stress will make us turn on one another."

Tree thought this over, biting her lip. "Well, in a way, it's worked for him. The crew is itchy and irritable. They're doing

their jobs, but it's almost like they're waiting for something bad
to happen. That's no way to live."

She turned the bike's torque up a notch, then gave Lita an ap-
preciative glance. "We've got to stick together." A few minutes
later, after grinding through two more miles, they both let their
bikes coast to a stop.

Lita wiped her head with a towel and said, "Okay, a shower
for me, and then an hour of piano practice. I'm getting it all done
in one shot tonight."

"I love listening to you play," Triana told her. "I'll pop in next
time if it's all right with you." She waved good-bye and headed
back to her room.

After a shower and a brief conversation with Roc—nothing
new to report, he said—she tumbled into bed and clasped her
hands behind her head. Within moments her thoughts turned
again to her dad. This time she recalled their rafting trip through
Brown's Canyon in Colorado. It had been early summer and the
water was running high, crashing into their boat as it hurtled
them along the canyon walls and past immense boulders. At one
point her dad lost his balance and nearly let the paddle slip from
his hands as he lurched for something to grab on to. Tree had
burst into a spasm of laughter, pulling her own oar out of the
water as she doubled over in a fit of joy. Their raft captain, a large
grizzled river veteran with no sense of humor, hollered over the
roar of the rapids, "Paddle! Paddle! Paddle!"

When they reached a somewhat gentler passage of the river,
everyone was able to take a break and recover their strength.

"You almost fell in," Tree had said, poking her oar into her
father's life vest.

"Yeah, well, I wasn't worried about the water. But those giant
rocks would have done a pretty good number on my head, even
with the helmet." Her dad had grinned back at her.

"I would have jumped in to save you," Tree said.

"I hope not," her dad said seriously. "In these waters you
wouldn't have a chance of reaching me. All you'd do is end up

hurting yourself, or worse." He put down his paddle and took a drink from his water bottle. "No, if I go in, you can try to reach me with your paddle, maybe give me something to grab on to. But if I'm sucked down the rapids, you have to save yourself."

Tree had thought this over for a moment. "You don't *want* me to try to save you?"

"Honey, you don't understand. If I'm lost, it doesn't do any good to risk killing yourself. Remember that, okay?"

Before she could reply, their captain had begun shouting orders again. They rushed into a new set of rapids, more deadly than the last group, and it was time to get back to work.

Now, three years later, staring at the ceiling in her room, Tree said the words aloud again. "I would have jumped in to save you."

Turning to her nightstand, she picked up the picture of her dad. "I guess I couldn't save you after all."

She studied his face, the wrinkles around his eyes, the strong chin, the smattering of gray hairs around his temples. She rolled over and raised herself up on one arm, looking across at her own image in the mirror. Then, casting a glance back at the photograph, she murmured, "I don't look very much like you. I look like . . . her." This troubled her. Softly, she ran a hand across his face.

"What did I get from you?"

A moment later she placed the picture back on the nightstand and lay back again, her hands behind her head.

"What exactly did I get from you?"

A faint beep came from her desk and broke her concentration. A call was coming through.

Arising with a sigh, she punched the intercom. "Yes?"

"Just thought I'd check in with you before hitting the sack," Gap said.

"Well, still nothing," she said. "I assume you're talking about the stowaway?"

"Yes and no. I'm also wondering how you're doing. You've

seemed . . . detached lately. That's the only word I can think of
right now. I wanted to know if there's something I can help
with."

"That's sweet of you," Tree said, smiling. "But everything's
fine. Just . . . missing my dad."

Gap was quiet for a few seconds. "I'm sorry. That's none of
my business."

"No, it's fine. It's part of your job on the Council to make sure
I'm in good shape physically and mentally."

"Well," Gap said, "I'm not really asking for professional reasons. I care about you as a person as much as a Council leader,
Tree."

Now it was her turn to sit quietly. Finally she started to speak
again. "Gap—"

"Listen," he said, "no big deal. Just making sure you're all
right. I'll see you in the morning, okay? Good night."

He broke the connection before she could say anything else.
She bit her lip and slouched in her chair. She had instantly re-
verted to her cold machine ways again, without even consider-
ing that someone might want to talk to her as a friend. Or as
more than that?

She shot another quick glance at her father's picture. "I know
what I *didn't* get from you, Dad. Obviously not your perception
or people skills."

Five minutes later she was back in bed, tossing and turning
briefly before dropping off to sleep. The hallway outside her door
was in night mode, the lights dimmed to a dusk setting. Without
a sound a figure glided up to her door, rested its hand on her
name panel briefly and then was gone.

28

M r. Scofield wants to know if he can have a moment with you."

Dr. Zimmer barely contained a groan. He waited for a few seconds before answering the page from the front desk operator. Putting off Scofield right now would only make the next confrontation with him that much more unbearable. Besides, *Galahad* was mere hours away from leaving. What could Scofield do now? Dr. Zimmer cringed at the thought, then cleared his voice and spoke up.

"All right, put him through."

He turned to the vidscreen behind his desk. This temporary office on the space station was cramped but had all the tools he needed to finish his work on the project.

The screen flickered for an instant before the haggard face of Tyler Scofield appeared. Dr. Zimmer noted that his adversary seemed to have aged a dozen years in the last two. He had also, like many who followed his belief of a return to a more simple life, grown a full beard. It did not, however, hide the weariness on his long, thin face.

"Hello, Wallace," he said.

"Hello, Tyler," Dr. Zimmer said. "I hate to be rude, but, as you can imagine, I've got my hands full right now. What can I do for you?"

"You have ignored my warnings, my advice, and my pleading," Scofield said.

"And your threats," Zimmer said.

"Your perception, Doctor, not my intent," came the stiff reply. "Since the day you proposed this ridiculous plan we have fought to show you the foolish mistake you are making. Now I ask for just one final opportunity, one last chance to persuade you to stop this madness."

Dr. Zimmer sighed. "*Galahad* will begin accelerating away from this station and from Earth in less than twelve hours. The crew is already aboard. Your feelings regarding the project have been obvious, Tyler, but perhaps now you might accept the fact that it's too late. *Galahad* will soon be gone. Why don't you take this final opportunity to wish them good luck?"

Scofield ignored this last question. "If you won't listen to our logical reasons for putting a halt to this, then why not consider the emotional reasons?"

"I've heard your—"

"You've heard, but you have not *listened!*" Scofield cried. "You have not listened to the cries of families who are losing their children at a time of personal tragedy. You have not listened to the anger and betrayal felt by millions of people who regard this folly as a sign that the human race has given up and is finished." He paused, his eyes blazing and his chest rising and falling with tortured breathing. He slowly composed himself, then pointed a finger at Zimmer and continued, this time with an icy calm.

"You have not listened to the message my organization has presented for more than two years, begging you to consider the psychological impact your project is having on the people— especially the children—who are staying put and fighting this horrible disease. No, you have not listened to anyone. Your selfish, obsessive 'vision' is the only thing that guides you, blinding you to the wisdom of anyone who dares to cross you, who dares to question you, who dares to say 'You are *wrong.*'"

Dr. Zimmer said nothing for a few moments while Scofield's

eyes stared through him. There were so many things that Zimmer wanted to say, so many fiery comebacks that were eager to spring from his lips. But he knew that would solve nothing. In fact, the things he *most* wanted to say would only make matters worse.

So he waited calmly, gathering his thoughts and his patience, measuring his words. When he finally spoke, his voice was strong and steady.

"Tyler, you and I were once good friends and colleagues. I have always held you in the warmest regard, which makes me very sorry that this tragedy has created such a deep chasm between us. I value my friendships, even more so during these last few years. Many things that seemed important before . . . well, they don't hold the power over me they once did. Friendships, however, do.

"But you know I am also passionate about the truth, Tyler. I will never allow my personal feelings to cloud my judgment when it comes to the truth. And the truth in this instance is undeniable. Comet Bhaktul has delivered a death sentence to our civilization as we know it. The facts are unpleasant, and that has caused many people to deny the truth. I am not surprised nor angry about this. Denial is a common human characteristic when we're faced with something we don't want to deal with. It's a form of mental protection. I understand that.

"And I understand why you are so strongly opposed to the *Galahad* project. To support this mission is to accept our own fatality. Few people are willing to do that."

He kept his gaze locked on to Scofield's. After a slight pause, his voice softened a bit.

"Tyler, I know what you are feeling. But we're both scientists. We can both read the data. And we can both predict the outcome. I have chosen to act in the best interests of our species. *That* is a basic human instinct as well: preservation of the species. Nobody would like to see Bhaktul's effects controlled and defeated any more than I. But the results are not there. And as each week and month passes, the window of opportunity closes a little more. Soon there will be no window at all. I can't let that happen. I *won't* let that happen, even if it costs me a friendship I treasure so strongly. I have to face the truth, Tyler, regardless of the pain involved."

For the first time Scofield's fierce stare lost its edge. His gaze fell down to his hands, clasped tightly in front of him.

"You are right," he said, "when you say that we were once friends. You were almost like a brother to me, and I, too, am sorry that we have grown so far apart. I suppose we were pushed apart by our own beliefs."

Scofield looked back up. "But you are wrong when it comes to *Galahad*. You said it was too late to do anything about it." He paused for one moment. "It's not too late, my old friend."

Dr. Zimmer's spine stiffened. The two men stared at each other, and just before the image faded to black, Scofield raised an eyebrow and repeated, "It's not too late."

29

Roc was cheating. Cheating, that was, as much as a programmed machine could. It was nine o'clock in the morning and he was engaged in his weekly game of Masego with Gap Lee.

The game had become very popular with the crew during their months of training. Nasha was a fifteen-year-old from Botswana in Africa who had fought her homesick feelings by teaching the game to a handful of crew members, and it quickly spread. Translated to English, the word meant "good luck," which was exactly what a player needed, as well as a razor-sharp mind.

The object involved moving three small marbles across various twisting paths on the board, then working them back one at a time without touching any of the spaces used on the initial trail. At the same time you had to block your opponent's return trip and force him onto a square forbidden to him. Each game was unique and exciting, and often led to whoops of celebration when someone claimed victory. An average game of Masego could run almost an hour, challenging your mind and testing your memory. Dr. Zimmer and Dr. Bauer had both loved it as a training tool; the kids loved it for the sheer competition.

Gap fancied himself to be one of the better players aboard *Galahad*. Nasha would smoke him regularly, but, as Gap was quick to point out, she had been playing since she was six or seven years old. So Gap always seemed to find himself playing against his favorite rival: Roc.

Once he had been "taught" the game by Nasha and programmed by Roy Orsini, Roc was supposed to play without using all of his computational skills. That was supposed to level the playing field against his human opponents. But, once again, too much of Roy's spirit found its way inside Roc. He loved to win. He also cheated. Gap was suspicious, but plugged on against the computer anyway with a weekly game. Gap would touch the screen with a finger to indicate his moves, and Roc would respond by lighting up his choice on the board.

Now, in the Conference Room, Gap sat in front of the vidscreen, his dark eyes fixed on the image of the playing board, his well-tuned mind racing through the possible combinations of the game.

"Your turn," Roc said.

"Mm-hmm," Gap mumbled.

"Would you like a suggestion?"

"No," Gap said. "I know how to play."

"Just trying to help. You've been sloppy in your moves today."

"Sloppy?"

"Sloppy," Roc said. "I picked up three spaces on your last move alone."

"Just let me play in peace," Gap said sullenly. "Nobody likes a gloater."

He was reaching out with a finger to place his next move when Roc piped up again.

"Are you sure about that?"

Gap pulled his finger back from the screen and instead jabbed it toward Roc's sensor.

"You know, you've gotten a little cockier since we left. Don't think just because Roy or Dr. Zimmer's not here that you can go wild. I know how to pull your plug, too, you know."

"Gap, what an awful thing to say."

"Just let me play. If I make a mistake, I'll learn from it."

"Hmm," Roc said. "If that was true you would be a Masego Grand Master by now."

Gap looked back at the board. "I'm not listening to you," he muttered. Then he quickly punched his selection onto the screen.

Without a second of delay Roc immediately lit up his next move on the board. Gap shifted his gaze back and forth across the layout, then sat back and sighed. His last move had opened up a new path for Roc that he hadn't noticed. Within three or four moves the game would be over.

"Care for another go?" Roc said with just a hint of sarcasm.

"Tomorrow," Gap said. "I don't like you very much right now."

He stood up and walked across the Conference Room to fill a glass with water. At that moment the door opened and Triana walked in.

"Thought I might find you here," she said.

"Yeah, well I wish I was somewhere else, actually," Gap said.

"Oh," Tree said. "I think I know what that means." She turned to the glowing red sensor. "Roc, why don't you let him win once in a while?"

"He says that losing helps him learn more," said Roc's cheerful voice.

"That's *not* what I said," Gap fumed. He looked at Tree with frustration etched on his face. "I'm not sure I can handle five more years with this box of attitude."

Tree couldn't hold her laughter any longer. In a way she felt sorry for Gap, who hated to lose. But at the same time she couldn't help laugh at the way Roc pushed Gap's hot buttons. Roy Orzini was most definitely alive and well inside his creation.

"Maybe you two should wait a while before you play Masego again," she said with a grin. "You don't play well together."

Gap didn't answer. He drank his water to camouflage his pouting. Roc, of course, had no problem responding.

"That might be best," the computer said. "I think all of the learning that Gap has done in our last ten games has clogged him up. He needs to let it drain a little."

Gap shook his head and looked at Tree. "See what I mean?"

Tree laughed again as the door opened and Bon, Channy and Lita walked in.

"What's so funny?" Channy said.

"Oh, just watching two boys poke at each other," Tree said.

The Council members all took seats around the table for their weekly meeting. After receiving updates from each and planning some new work schedules, they turned to new business. Nothing important, it seemed. A few crew members were requesting new roommate assignments.

"We figured that would happen," Lita said. "It's one thing to pick a roomie during training. After you live with them a few weeks you learn a lot more. I'm surprised there aren't more requests like this."

Tree okayed the changes and asked Lita to handle it.

Channy and Bon had nothing new. Bon was fidgeting, as usual, anxious to get out of the meeting and back to work.

"Wait a minute," Tree said when it looked like things were wrapping up. "I have some news."

The group got quiet. Tree bit her lip for a second, then looked up at them.

"When I checked my e-mail this morning," she said, "there was a note from our . . . passenger."

"What?" Gap burst out. "And you're just now telling us?"

"I wanted to take care of all the other business first," Tree said.

While the others sat in shock, Bon spoke up. "What did he say?"

Tree tapped her fingers on the tabletop. "Well, he wants to meet with me. Alone."

Channy put a hand to her mouth. "Oh, no. Are you serious?"

Tree said, "Yeah. But he was very vague. No specifics. Just a note that said 'Let's talk.'"

"How do you know it was him?" Lita said. "How did he sign it?"

"He didn't. But it was him," Tree said. "I checked the source of the e-mail. It came from one of the terminals in the Dining Hall. Sent about two o'clock this morning."

"He likes to drift through the ship after everyone has gone to bed," Channy said. "This guy gives me the creeps."

Triana slowly let out her breath. "So, we need to discuss how we want to handle this."

Gap stared at her with his mouth agape. "Don't tell me you're thinking about meeting him alone," he said slowly. "That's just crazy."

"I don't know," Bon said. "What better way to find out who he is and what he wants?"

"Yeah, and what better way to get Tree killed!" yelled Gap, shooting Bon a fiery glance.

"I'm sorry, but I have to agree with Gap," Lita said. "Tree, I can't believe you would even consider that. We have no idea who this person is. All we know is that he has caused damage already on this ship and threatened the entire crew. Meeting him alone would be just plain stupid."

"She's right," Channy said. "Tree, you're the Council Leader. You don't just go marching off into battle alone."

"Okay," Bon said, "but why would he ask to meet with her? If he wanted to hurt her, wouldn't he just wait until he found her alone? Why would he put her on alert like that? Maybe he really does just want to talk."

Gap was seething. He stood up and leaned across the table towards Bon.

"You make me sick," he said. "Try to think of someone else for a change, Bon. If you're that anxious for us to make contact with him, maybe you should volunteer to meet him alone yourself."

"Hold on a minute," Tree said.

"I'm not sure you belong on this Council anymore," Gap shouted at Bon, who glared back.

"Well isn't it too bad that's not your decision," Bon said.

"That's enough!" Tree said, slamming her hand down on the table. "Gap, sit down."

Gap remained still for a few more seconds. He looked as if he wanted to climb over the table and tangle with the sullen Swede. Finally he sat back down, but didn't take his eyes off Bon.

Tree resumed control of the meeting. "I appreciate everyone's comments and opinions," she said, her voice still strong and loud. "The purpose of this Council is to share thoughts and ideas to help *Galahad* run smoothly. I don't expect everyone to agree with every suggestion. But—"

She looked back and forth between the two boys, who were staring each other down.

"But I don't expect this Council to break down during debate, either. If you two can't carry out the tasks expected of you without resorting to violence, then neither of you belongs here."

With this, Gap looked at Tree, back at Bon, then down at the table. Bon took a deep breath and broke his gaze as well.

"Lita predicted this would happen," Tree said in a softer tone. "This intruder is winning when we turn on each other, rather than focus on him. When we collapse as a team we give him an advantage. I don't want to do that. Do you?"

"You're right," Gap said. "But this is a serious issue."

"And that's exactly why you were selected by Dr. Zimmer in the first place," Tree said. "Leadership is defined by how you perform during tough times. Anyone can lead during good times."

Lita spoke up. "If I could make a suggestion?"

"Sure," Tree said.

"Why not invite our mystery man to a Council meeting? If we promise him that no harm will come to him, he might agree to talk with all of us."

"I don't know," Channy said doubtfully. "This guy is probably infected with Bhaktul Disease. He's not going to be rational, and it wouldn't be smart—or safe—for us to assume that he would be. That could get someone killed."

"Channy's right," Bon said. "He's not going to talk to us rationally. He's sick. We need to track him down."

"And then?" Gap said. "We don't have a jail on this ship."

"I don't know," Bon said. "But for now we should take it one step at a time. Let's find him, see how dangerous he really is, and go from there. I don't want him loose much longer, that's for sure. He's already proved that he can destroy at will. If we wait and allow Bhaktul to progress even further, he might just cripple this ship. Which is why," he said, looking back at Gap, "I think it might make sense for Tree to meet with him. Yes, he could be dangerous. But a week from now he's going to be even more dangerous."

Gap was about to respond when Tree cut in.

"I'm going to send a copy of the e-mail to all of you. Take a look and see if there's anything in it that I'm not seeing. Oh, and Roc?"

"Yes?" the computer said.

"I'm also sending a copy to you. I'd like to get your opinion as well."

"Okay," Roc said. "I've been thinking about everything that's happened so far. The text of his note might support a few thoughts I have."

Lita looked up sharply. "What does that mean? What kind of thoughts?"

"Yeah," Gap said, "do you think you might know who this is?"

"Part of my programming did involve deductive reasoning," Roc said. "And I've read every Sherlock Holmes story ever written. Unfortunately we don't have a lot to work with. Good detectives would tell you that it's dangerous to jump ahead without facts. But let's say I'm taking steps with each new development. Can't wait to see the e-mail, Tree."

She looked around at the Council. "Are there any other questions or comments?"

"I'll save mine," Bon said, rising to his feet. "They apparently cause strong emotional reactions from some people."

Without making eye contact with anyone he strode quickly from the room. Gap shook his head in disgust, but bit his tongue.

The others stood to leave. As they began to file out, Triana touched Gap's arm and motioned for him to stay behind.

When they were alone she said to him, "Listen, I just want to say a couple of things, okay? First, thanks for what you said in this meeting. I know that you really care about what happens to me, and that . . . that means a lot. Not many people have ever felt that way about me."

Gap looked down sheepishly, but didn't say anything.

"And I want to say I'm sorry about last night, too," she continued. "You were just being a friend, and I was . . . well, I was pretty cold. I guess I'm just not used to that from anyone but my dad."

He made eye contact with her when he felt her touch his arm again. Her eyes were slightly moist. Suddenly he felt embarrassed putting her through this.

"Tree—" he said.

"I'm going to try to be a better friend, Gap. You deserve it."

They were alone in the room, their eyes locked, and her hand resting slightly on his arm. Gap's mind was racing, an internal debate raging.

Sorry, I've got to break in here. Remember that talk we had about hormones? I'm watching this beautiful scene in the Conference Room and I want to scream at Gap: Kiss her, you idiot! Kiss her! Right on the mouth! It doesn't have to be a long, drawn-out thing. Just a quick "how-do-you-do, I'm putting my mouth on yours and what do you think of that?"

Gee, I hate to coach the guy, and I can't really speak up, but c'mon! Who knows, she might kiss him back. Yes, the crew is in turmoil and, yes, it looks like some crazy nut is hiding out on the ship, and yes, the carpet in this Conference Room is completely tacky, but c'mon! If ever you had the chance, Gap, this is it. You can do it!

Gap hesitated, and in that time Triana let go of his arm and stepped around him to the door. Suddenly he was alone.

With his heart pounding he realized he'd been holding his breath. He sat down dejectedly, exhaling, and rested his head on one hand.

"Idiot," he muttered. "Idiot, idiot, idiot."

You've got to be kidding me. All right, enough of this. There must be some report I should be working on right now.

alahad had been gone for more than a week. With most of his follow-up work either finished or on schedule, Wallace Zimmer was packing for home. Just as well, he thought; the sooner he was off this antiseptic space station and back among greenery the better. He amused himself by plotting his first real meal in weeks. Lobster, he decided, with a side dish of steaming pasta and vegetables.

The thought brightened his spirits slightly, which helped him pick up the pace of activity. His preparations to leave had been hampered by the creeping fatigue that was one of the curses of Bhaktul Disease. Ten minutes of any physical exertion now had to be followed by five or ten minutes of rest. The coughing spasms were also coming more frequently. On one level it was distressing, simply because it meant that the illness was gaining momentum within him. But it also angered the proud scientist; he had taken great pains to keep himself in good physical shape throughout his life and to be overpowered by a microscopic particle was maddening.

At this particular moment he felt weary. Into one of his large briefcases he tossed an old, worn notebook. In his office at home there were several others just like it. They were crammed with personal notes and feelings from the entire *Galahad* mission, starting with the selection process and finishing with the successful launch. More than two years' worth of observations and memories, crammed into a series of old-fashioned notebooks. Some were held together with tape, all of them were a mishmash of scribbled paragraphs, scratched out sentences, arrows that referred forwards and backwards through the pages, and hastily added notes in the margins.

His computer work pad kept all of the official project notes and information; these pen and paper collections housed the tears and tales that never made it into the official reports. To anyone else they would be practically illegible, but to Dr. Zimmer it was a clear, concise description of the most important endeavor mankind had ever pulled off.

As soon as he returned to Earth he would begin to transcribe it all into a book. No matter what the outcome of the human population, it was imperative that a full account survive.

Closing the briefcase, he plopped down into the chair behind his desk. After a few deep breaths he snapped on his e-mail monitor and checked for any urgent messages. There were none, which made him both happy and sad.

Happy because it meant that *Galahad* was still running smoothly and apparently without trouble, regardless of Roc's inquiries about the energy balance. Sad, however, because it was further evidence that the baby bird had flown from the nest for good. He wanted more than anything for the kids to be safe and secure, but in a perverse way he had hoped that they would somehow still need him for something.

It was the Council that had insisted on the no contact decree. Once the ship was safely away and the solar wings deployed, radio contact would cease. Roc would continue to relay some information on a daily basis, mostly to confirm course and direction, but that would be it. No calls home, the Council had decided. "What good would it do, really?" Lita had said. "We have to become independent as quickly as possible, and clinging on to Earth's apron won't help us do that."

Yet Dr. Zimmer had secretly hoped for one more call. It didn't look like it was going to happen.

31

Regardless of what Gap, Lita and Channy thought, Tree had already made up her mind. In fact, she had made up her mind long before Bon had suggested she meet the stowaway. She had made that decision as soon as she read his note.

She stood alone near the entrance to the Dining Hall, watching about three dozen crew members carrying their lunch trays and congregating at the tables in groups of three or four. The din in the room grew as more kids trickled in, greetings were exchanged and the tables began to fill up.

Several of the crew members stopped as they entered and chatted briefly with Triana. They made the usual small talk, asking how she was, how things were going, then said good-bye and sauntered over to the food dispensers. But none of them mentioned the intruder to Triana. That seemed to be a subject that was too uncomfortable for the casual atmosphere of their lunch break.

That was okay with her. After the stormy Council meeting she was only too happy to confine her conversations to more mundane topics. Besides, she realized that many of her shipmates felt a little awkward talking with her anyway, as if they were unsure what to say to their ship's leader. This was a feeling quite familiar to Triana. Social skills had never been her strongest suit.

After glancing around the room one more time she noted that the one person she was interested in talking to hadn't arrived yet. A quick check of the work schedule had told her that he should be part of this late lunch group, but apparently he was running behind. Triana finally decided to wait for him at a table.

Picking up a tray she stood in line at the dark gray dispensers, slowly moving along and keeping an eye on the door. Each time it opened she would look up to see who had entered, then continue to shuffle along.

A special treat greeted her when it was her turn. The usual plate of processed energy blocks was garnished with several chunks of actual fruit. She smiled as she noticed slices of apple, pear and bananas adorning one section of the plate. It seemed the crops were ahead of schedule. Bon had mentioned to the Council that it might be another week before their first fruit was ready, but she was delighted to see that today was the day.

Bon was infuriating at times, but he knew his stuff when it came to farming, she admitted to herself. Why did he have to make it so hard to like him?

Picking up her tray after filling a glass with water, Triana turned to look for a quiet spot to sit down. At that moment the door opened and Peter Meyer walked in with two other guys. All three were working a shift in the Agricultural Center and Triana could see remnants of dirt and dust on the knees of their pants. They made their way towards the stack of trays. Triana altered her path to intercept them.

"Hello, Peter," she said, causing him to glance over at her. His two companions grew quiet.

"Hi," Peter said.

"Listen, when you get your lunch would you mind stopping by my table over there for just a minute? I'm sorry to interrupt, but I want to ask you something."

Peter's face conveyed a "what have I done now?" look. He shrugged and said, "Sure."

Triana carried her lunch over to a vacant table in the corner. She was pretty sure she would have it to herself until Peter sat down.

She was enjoying the fresh fruit when the Canadian plopped his tray across from her and pulled out a chair.

"This was a pleasant surprise," she said to him, indicating the apple slice in her hand.

"Yeah, we finished harvesting the first few bushels yesterday," Peter said. "Instead of an announcement we thought it would be better just to surprise everyone. Now that everything's up and running smoothly we should have a fairly constant supply."

"I love it," Triana said. "When the oranges are ready I'll just about have a cow."

Peter smiled. "Well, you should start feeling the labor pains in two weeks or so," he said.

Triana finished her apple and watched Peter as he spread his lunch out on the table. The last time she had seen him was during the frenzy in Sick House. Now, instead of panic, his manner was one of curiosity. She felt bad that she had dragged him away from his friends, and knew that everyone had watched him make his way over to sit with her. Undoubtedly he would be subjected to endless questions later.

"I hope you don't mind," she said, "but I want to talk with you about that day near the Storage Section."

Peter's face clouded and he nervously pushed his now empty tray out of the way. Picking up his fork he speared a chunk of energy block. "Okay," he said finally.

"For one thing," Triana said, "You told us he said something like, 'Are you ready to die?' Do you remember him saying anything else?"

Peter sat still for a moment, chewing his food. His brow wrinkled as he thought.

"I . . . I really don't remember," he told her. "I don't think so."

Triana nodded. "What was he doing when you saw him? Was he just walking along, or was he standing there?"

"Well, he was just standing there when I came around the corner. His back was to me, and he was pretty much in the shadows, but . . ."

"But what?"

"Well . . . I can't be sure, but I think he had just stood up. Like he had been down on one knee or something."

Triana digested this for a minute. As she took her last bite of fruit she looked back up at Peter.

"So he obviously heard you coming around the corner. Maybe you startled him. Maybe . . . maybe interrupted him from something."

"I don't know. Maybe."

"Hmm," Triana said, deep in thought. What would an intruder have been doing on the floor in that section?

"Peter, where exactly did you see him? I mean, exactly where in that section?"

"Well, I was coming up on the window around the corner from the lift. I was trying to get a view of the moon, and I knew that there was a big window in that hallway, the one just before you get to the Spider bay. I can't say exactly, but I'd guess I was maybe halfway between the lift and the observation window."

That coincided with the area where Gap had found the coin. Perhaps Peter had indeed startled the intruder and caused him to accidentally drop the quarter. But what was he doing there?

"All right, thanks Peter," she said. She was about to get up when she decided to ask him one more question. On an impulse she said, "By the way, are you familiar with a man named Tyler Scofield?"

"I know the name," Peter said slowly. "I don't know if I've ever seen him before. Isn't he the guy who was so against *Galahad*?"

"Yeah," Triana sighed. "He and Dr. Zimmer used to be good friends."

"Is that who you think is on board?" Peter said. "You think he's trying to sabotage the ship?"

"I don't know," Triana said. "Maybe. It all fits. The beard, the fact that he was so against this mission. Even the coin."

"The coin? How?"

Triana bit her lip for a moment. Then she said, "Well, I never met the man face-to-face. But I saw a vidclip of him about three months before we went into the Incubator. Almost sinister looking is how I'd describe him. He was giving a speech about *Galahad*, about how Dr. Zimmer was playing a game of chance with people's children.

"At one point he pulled something out of his pocket and flipped it in the air and caught it. He kept saying 'Heads or tails. Heads or tails.' I didn't know what it meant. He said it was something that people his age would understand."

"So what did it mean?" Peter said, gazing intently at *Galahad*'s Council leader.

"I asked Dr. Zimmer. He just waved it off and said not to worry about it. You know, he never wanted us to get distracted from our training. So later I asked Dr. Armistead."

"And?"

"She said it meant a fifty-fifty chance. She said when people still used coins for money they would flip them and bet on which side came up. You had a fifty-fifty chance of winning.

"Apparently Scofield was angry, and believed that Dr. Zimmer was gambling with people's families, that his plan was a long shot, no better than a game of chance. Scofield handed out coins to his followers to . . . I don't know, inspire them to defeat the mission. Dr. Armistead said that Scofield wanted to make it a symbol of how desperate our chances were. It never caught on, though."

Peter shrugged. "I never saw that. Like I said, I heard his name before, but I must not have heard about the coins."

"Listen, do you think you could recognize him if Roc pulled up a picture of Scofield?" Triana said.

"I don't know. I didn't get a very good look at him. I was . . .

pretty freaked out, I guess." Peter lowered his face, ashamed of the memory.

Triana touched his hand lightly. "Hey, don't worry about it. I would have freaked out, too. Any of us would have."

Peter nodded, but kept his head down.

"Well, do me a favor," Triana said. "When you're finished with lunch stop by the Conference Room and have Roc pull up a photo of Scofield. Just check it out. It can't hurt to try. And let me know later, okay?"

"Sure," Peter said.

Late that afternoon a sizable crowd had gathered to watch the opening of the three-on-three soccer tournament. For a while there had been discussions about postponing it until their intruder issue was resolved. But Channy was insistent that they not buckle under his intimidation.

"Listen, he might be sneaking around, writing scary memos on the walls and kicking up a few clods in the farm, but he's not going to ruin our fun. No way. Let the games begin."

And so they did. Thirty teams, almost half of the ship's population, had signed up for this three-day tournament. Each team fielded three players at a time, with one extra who subbed. The games were played on fields much smaller than the kids were used to back home, but space inside *Galahad* was very much at a premium. This time around, however, Zimmer didn't need much convincing. He could relate to soccer much more easily than Airboarding. Two fields were squeezed together inside one large room on the second level.

With the smaller playing fields the action was much more intense and the scoring much higher. And, since the crew members on *Galahad* were naturally more competitive than the average teen, the physical aspect of the games was compounded, as well. This was definitely a contact sport.

Channy was in charge, but took time out in the early evening to sit for a few minutes with Gap and Lita in the stands. They kept their eyes on the match in front of them while they discussed the latest Council meeting.

"I just find it interesting that she kept this note from the stowaway to herself until the end of the meeting," Channy said. "If I get a note from this guy I'm not waiting two seconds to let someone know about it."

Lita put her fingers into her mouth and whistled loudly at a great save by one of the players on the field. "But it's just like Tree, if you think about it. She doesn't get worked up about anything, really. I can totally see her sitting on that note until she thought it was the right time to talk about it."

"Yeah, maybe," Gap said. "But doesn't it make you wonder if she's telling us everything?"

Channy took her eyes off the game and stared at him. "You think she knows more than she's telling us? That doesn't make any sense."

"I don't know," Gap said, unconvinced. "Look, she's a loner for the most part anyway, right? C'mon, don't look at me like that, we all know she is. And that's fine. Personally, I'd like to get to know her a little better, but I respect her decision to keep mostly to herself. But doesn't that make you wonder if sometimes she thinks she can handle something by herself?"

Lita thought about this, then looked quizzically at Gap. "What are you saying? That she's gonna try to track down this guy alone?" Her face contorted into a look of disbelief. "That's ridiculous, Gap. She weighs about one hundred ten pounds. She's not gonna try to take him on."

"No, but she probably isn't thinking about a physical confrontation," Gap said. "Tree is one of the smartest people on this ship . . . and there's a lot of smart people crammed in here. I just get the feeling that she thinks she can outsmart this guy. You know, brains over brawn, that old cliché."

"So why would she try to do that by herself?" Channy said. "She doesn't think we're smart enough to help her?"

"No, that's not it," Gap said. All three of the Council members instinctively threw their hands up as one of the soccer players deflected the ball up into the bleachers. It was grabbed by a girl two rows in front of them, and everyone relaxed again.

"No," Gap said again. "I don't think she feels that way at all. It's just . . ." He paused, trying to figure out the right words to express himself. "It's just that she's so independent, and feels so much pressure, I think, to lead this mission, that she thinks she has to take on all the responsibility herself. It's not that she doesn't like the help. I just think she doesn't like asking for it."

"Well, that actually makes sense," Lita said. "I've talked with her enough to know that she grew up that way. She absolutely worshipped her dad, and when he died she kinda felt like she didn't have anybody else to rely on. She's had that spirit since we've all known her, you know what I mean? Like, 'I can do this by myself,' that kinda thing."

"What if we talked to her about it?" Channy said. "Told her that she doesn't have to solve every problem alone?"

"Or, don't say anything and just start volunteering to help her more," Lita suggested. "We're not going to change her personality, I don't think. It's better if we just showed our support and let her figure it out for herself."

Gap nodded. "I just hope she doesn't get herself into trouble in the meantime."

A cheer rose from the crowd as another goal was scored.

L isten, I know I'm a little bit of an attention hog, but I'll be honest with you.

I don't feel too good.

There's nothing wrong with the ship, at least that I can tell. The life-support systems are okay, the gravity system is perfect, the crops are growing, the water recycling unit is good. . . .

But something's not right with me.

I was talking with Bon in the Farm Dome when it first happened.

I . . . well, I guess I blacked out. One moment I'm hearing everything that Bon is saying, and the next thing I know I'm out of it. Must have lasted about ten seconds. Bon asked what had happened, and I quite honestly couldn't tell him. He shrugged it off as a fluke of some kind, but I'm not so sure. In all my years of programming and testing, nothing like that has ever happened.

It was like a human losing consciousness. Their heart keeps beating, their lungs continue to breathe, but the signal with the outside world is cut off momentarily. Very puzzling.

I haven't run a full diagnostic test on myself for a couple of months. Must be time.

And then there's the matter of our uninvited guest. I've gone through every detail over and over again, and there's one answer that keeps popping up.

I think it's time to talk with Tree about it. After my test, of course.

32

The passenger section on the shuttle was practically empty. Wallace Zimmer knew that the staff on the space station had begun to thin out within hours of the departure of *Galahad*. When he had finally decided to head back to Earth he left behind a crew of perhaps only two dozen orbiting in the space lab.

He flipped on the vidscreen built into the seatback ahead of him and selected an all-news station. What greeted him was mostly depressing: a reporter stood before a vacant office building in the United States, reflecting on the slow but continuous demise of most businesses. There were too many people ill, and those that were as yet unaffected by the disease were unable to keep up with the workload. Another report from Western Europe showed images of rioting, as hordes of frightened people took out their frustration on a pharmacy that had shut its doors rather than turn away people desperate for medicinal help.

That was the problem: there was no help from the medical front in the foreseeable future. Doctors and scientists were still at a loss to explain exactly how Bhaktul worked on its human hosts. While there were some similarities in each case, such as coughing and severe headaches, often madness at the end, there were also hundreds of different symptoms. It was as if Bhaktul took different paths, threading its way through each person at a different vulnerable point. That made containment—and any possible antidote—incredibly difficult to provide.

Flipping the channel he gazed at a newscast photo of Tyler Scofield. Zimmer adjusted the volume up slightly and listened as the news anchor announced that Scofield's headquarters had also gone dark. No one had seen the renowned scientist in more than a week, and it was assumed that the launch of *Galahad* had sent Scofield into hiding somewhere. There was a quick mention of the spacecraft picking up speed on its way towards Saturn, and how it would use the giant gas planet's gravitational pull for a slingshot effect into deep space. Then the station broke for a commercial.

Sighing, Dr. Zimmer shut off the vidscreen and glanced out the tiny window beside his seat, scanning the image of the blue-green planet that rotated lazily below him. It looked peaceful and undisturbed, like a child curled up asleep. Soft clouds glided above the surface, and sunlight dappled off the water. He was amazed at the deception, how the gentle appearance concealed the despair that weaved its way throughout the population. This would be his last view of Earth from space, he realized with a start, which only deepened his sadness.

A coughing spasm made him convulse suddenly, and the taste of blood was stronger than before. He pulled out a tissue and dabbed his mouth, noticing the tiny spots of red before he returned the tissue to his pocket.

Straightening up, he plugged his work pad into the connection beneath the vidscreen and proceeded to access his mail. A few more scattered congratulations from colleagues around the world, along with a short note from his doctor. It mentioned a new cough suppressant that helped ease the pain that might accompany the intense spasms Zimmer had reported to him. "And," the note added, "it has also been shown to decrease the likelihood of coughing up blood, although you haven't mentioned that happening with you. For future reference, though . . ."

Dr. Zimmer grimaced. He hadn't mentioned it, of course. "At

my next appointment," he kept saying to himself. He wondered if it was too late for the drug to help.

With almost two hours to go before landing in California, he decided to spend the time writing to some of the people closest to him. He wrote a long letter to his only surviving sister and another to his half brother. Both letters apologized for his lack of attention to them over these last two years. He hoped they understood how the *Galahad* project had dominated his time. He wished them well, asked about their spouses and children, and closed with a reference to his own declining health. As he read over the letters before pushing the send button, he noted that he was really composing good-bye letters. They weren't eloquent, but he hoped they conveyed his love.

He sent another thank-you note to Angela Armistead. She had cried to the point of making herself sick when the door to *Galahad* had sealed shut. Dr. Zimmer had hugged her for a long time, feeling the grief that wracked her body. Barely thirty years old when the project began, she had come to feel that each of the star travelers was like a brother or sister to her. Zimmer hoped that she found peace quickly.

Next he wrote a brief note to Dr. Bauer, thanking him once again for his two years of work on the project. "I know that you sacrificed time that could have been spent with your family. I don't know how others would regard that commitment; some would call it despicable while others might call it honorable. I just wanted you to know how much I appreciate what you did. There are 251 young people who echo those sentiments. They carry a part of you with them to the stars."

Dr. Zimmer included warm wishes to Bauer's family. He started to ask about Fenton Bauer's relationship with his son, but decided that it probably would not be appropriate. "I'm sure it feels good to be home," he closed. "When you find a spare moment, please give me a call. I would love to visit with you again."

His final letter was to Tyler Scofield. "No matter our differences over the issue that has occupied our lives the last two years, I want you to know how much I continue to respect you and your convictions. I'll always treasure the friendship that kept us bonded for many years, and want you to know that those memories will be the ones that take priority when my thoughts turn to you."

And he meant it. Scofield had fought him at every step during the entire project, and hurtful barbs had been thrown in both directions. But Wallace Zimmer was now at peace, and truly hoped that his old friend-turned-adversary felt the same.

Before sending the e-mail he considered the news story that mentioned Scofield's disappearance. He hoped the acclaimed scientist would still be checking his messages, wherever he had gone.

Zimmer sent a handful of other quick notes to his rather small circle of close friends and associates. His final task was a mass e-mail of congratulations and thanks to each of the hundreds and hundreds of people who had devoted their precious time and energy to the success of *Galahad*. "You have made a difference, one that we won't ever be able to witness ourselves, but will ripple across the galaxy over time. In a time of despair and sadness, let that one thought lift your spirits. You are all heroes."

He unplugged his work pad and put it away. The time had flown during his writing, and touchdown on the desert runway was now only ten minutes away. The weary scientist closed his eyes, leaned back in his chair, and waited.

he hallways of *Galahad* were quiet. It was almost midnight and most of the exhausted crew slept. The three-day soccer tournament had ended that evening, the winning team claiming victory with a last-second goal in the championship game. "I couldn't have scripted a better ending to our first tournament," Channy had exclaimed to the cheering throng gathered on the field. The spirit of the crew was high.

Before turning in, Triana had congratulated the winners on the ship's vidscreens and also thanked Channy for all of her hard work. "We've trained hard for this mission, we work hard each day to sustain ourselves," she said. "But balance is crucial to our mental well-being. We will always play as hard as we work. Let's never lose that edge."

She had made a couple of other quick announcements regarding possible shift changes in the coming days, and reminded each crew member to check their personal e-mail at least twice a day.

Now, as midnight approached, Triana prepared for bed. Kicking off her slippers, she brushed her teeth and laid out her favorite T-shirt to sleep in. Then, sitting at her desk, she flipped open her journal and began to write.

I keep replaying my conversation with Peter Meyer, and now all I can see in my mind is Tyler Scofield creeping along the corridors of the ship. It's true he wanted to disrupt the mission, but is he the type of person who would resort to violence to destroy the ship and the crew?

Triana couldn't answer that question. For one thing, she had never met the man. Second, there was no telling what the ravages of Bhaktul might have done to his mental state. And third, what if it wasn't him? The description fit, but unfortunately she wasn't ready to declare Scofield the intruder. Peter had been unable to positively identify him from the pictures Roc had available. The young Canadian had only glimpsed the man in the Storage Section. The beard was roughly the same, he said, but something just wasn't clicking. All of Roc's photos were several years old, and time or disease could have altered the man's appearance. Triana felt as frustrated as ever.

If we don't catch him soon I'm going to rethink my decision about opening the Storage Sections. Roc is working on it, and I'm willing to give it one more day or two. After that we go on the attack; I'm tired of waiting for this person—whoever it is—to show himself.

She wasn't particularly tired yet, so rather than shutting off the light in her room and climbing into bed, she flicked on her vidscreen and checked a graphic that showed the location of *Galahad* within the solar system. Their track was holding steady on a course that would shoot them past the orbit of Mars and on towards Saturn. She scanned ahead and eyed the future path of the massive ship as it rocketed towards the outer planets. Their final contact with human life would come briefly near Saturn. There, an orbiting research station with a crew of thirty scientists would share radio contact with *Galahad* and check on their status. That team would then relay a final report back to Earth, acknowledging the passing of the vessel on its way out of the solar system. Triana did not necessarily look forward to that communication. It would seem like another good-bye, which she dreaded.

After that, appearing on her screen as a weak point of light, was Eos. Between them, several light-years of inky blackness, and the great unknown.

After pausing for another moment, Triana clicked open her e-mail.

And immediately let out her breath in a gasp.

It was another note from the stowaway. The subject line read "Time to exchange a handshake." After hesitating briefly, she slowly clicked open the letter and began to read.

Greetings again, Ms. Martell. I extend to you an invitation to join me for a lively discussion on the future of your assignment. I know that you must have several questions, and it will be my pleasure to answer as many of those as possible.

By now I'm sure you have discussed my first letter with your fellow Council members, and I'm equally sure that they have counseled you to refrain from meeting alone with me. If I read you correctly, you have not reached this same conclusion. My impression is that you prefer to handle matters yourself. I appreciate that. It has always been my way, as well.

Tonight would be an excellent opportunity for us to exchange a handshake and get to know each other better. I'm quite confident that after you hear my thoughts, you'll wonder why you were ever so concerned. Please allow me the chance to put your mind at ease.

I will wait for you in the Storage Section of the ship between midnight and 12:30 A.M. That should give us the peace and quiet that we need to seriously discuss matters. I doubt that we'll be disturbed at that time of the morning.

Again, I respectfully request that you come alone. If I
see more than just your bright young face, I will disap-
pear, and this offer will not be repeated. Do we understand each other? If you do not come alone, you will miss
your one and only chance to visit with me.

If you do not appear by 12:30, I will assume that you
refuse this meeting, and I will move on to my next task. A
task, I might add, that you will find most distressing, to
say the least.

Until then, Ms. Martell, I bid you good night.

Triana reread the note, biting her lip. She glanced quickly at
the clock in the top corner of her vidscreen: 12:02 A.M.

Her mind raced. It would only take a few minutes to reach
the Storage Section of *Galahad,* which allowed her time to
make the appointment. It did not necessarily give her time to
contact the members of the Council and collect their opinions.
Besides, she already knew that their answers wouldn't be any
different from the last time. And this intruder, whoever he was,
had now eerily threatened further damage, a threat that Triana
took very seriously. In her judgment a private meeting was better than leaving him to possibly cripple their ship.

Well, she had just expressed a desire to go on the attack.
Now, it seemed, was her only chance.

She stood up to change back into her clothes, then had a sudden thought. Sitting back down, she snapped on her vidscreen
audio and called out, "Roc?" It made sense to her to at least tell
the computer what was happening. Somebody needed to know
what her plans were, and Roc would be able to convey the message to the other Council members later, should anything go
wrong.

But there was no answer from Roc. The audio speaker remained silent. "Roc?" she said again. Still silence.

Now Triana was more troubled than ever. She wondered if
the threat mentioned by this intruder involved somehow dis-

rupting communication with *Galahad*'s master computer. He had said that Triana had until 12:30. It was now 12:03.

With her heart racing, she changed back into her everyday work clothes and started to race out into the hallway, pausing only briefly to glance at the picture of her father beside her bed. "Help me, Dad," she said softly, and then broke into a run out the door.

A t that moment Gap was in his room, leaning back in a chair. His feet, clad only in socks, were propped up on the table, his shoes tossed haphazardly to the side. A blanket his mother had made was wrapped around his upper body, more as a comfort piece than a practical tool for keeping warm. His eyelids were heavy, and occasionally his chin would bob onto his chest, jerking him back to attention. After one particularly long yawn he stretched his arms upwards, trying to fight off the urge to sleep. He was exhausted. After a quick glance at the clock on the vidscreen he figured about another hour and he would be able to fall into bed.

His roommate, Daniil Temka, was sleeping soundly across the room. That didn't help much, either.

For the third night in a row he had kept up this vigil. On the vidscreen before him was a live security camera shot. It was focused on the hallway at the end of this particular section of residential quarters. Through the dim light Gap was able to watch the last fifteen feet of hallway and the entrance to the lift. His eyes never left the vidscreen for more than a few seconds, which only made the task of remaining awake that much more difficult.

Yet he was determined to stay awake each night and keep watch over the hallway and the lift. If his hunch was right, Triana would not report her next message from the secretive stowaway. She was more likely to accept his offer to meet, which meant putting herself into more danger than she probably realized.

Gap would not let that happen. He reasoned that Triana would be asleep by one o'clock each night at the latest, so it shouldn't be that difficult to keep watch for a little while. If by one there was no sign, then he was confident she wouldn't be sneaking off to a private rendezvous. It just so happened that he was particularly tired this night. The time dragged.

Suddenly an image flashed across the vidscreen. Gap shot upright in the chair, his blanket falling to the floor. He leaned forward and looked closely at the screen. It was Triana.

She raced up to the lift door, waving a hand over the sensor. In a matter of seconds the door opened and she scampered inside. It closed just as quickly, and she was gone. It had all lasted less than ten seconds.

Gap sat stunned. He had watched for this, anticipating that it could happen. But he was still unprepared for it. His action plan wasn't exactly complete. It had allowed for keeping watch; it hadn't really included what to do after that. His thoughts tumbled into one another, backing up and slowing his reaction time.

Snapping out of his frozen trance, he punched in the code that would open an audio link to Lita's room. At the same time he reached for his shoes under the table. A light tone sounded, signaling a connection to his fellow Council member.

"Lita!" he called out. "Lita, wake up. It's Gap."

He fumbled with his shoes, slipping them on and snapping them shut all in one movement. "C'mon Lita, wake up."

"Mmmh," he heard her mumble through the speaker. "What?"

"Listen, it's me. You gotta wake up and call the others. Tree is on the move."

"What are you talking about? What time is it?"

"A little after twelve. C'mon, snap out of it. Tree is on the move."

Lita's voice sounded sluggish. "Yeah, I heard that. What do you mean? On the move where?"

"Listen, there's no time for this. Tree just tore out of her room, and I know she's going to meet up with the stowaway. Just wake up the others and meet me . . ." Gap trailed off, his mind racing. That was a good question, now wasn't it? Meet where?

"Meet where?" Lita said at the same time he was thinking it.

He stopped, glancing back at the monitor that now showed an empty hallway in front of the lift.

"Meet me in the Storage Section. Hurry up!"

He snapped off the intercom without waiting for a reply. Pushing back from the chair he called out, "Roc!"

There was no answer. Daniil had awakened and was propped up on one arm, trying to comprehend what the commotion was all about.

"Roc!" Gap tried again, leaning towards the red sensor.

Silence.

"Oh, no," he said under his breath. Without waiting to investigate, he scrambled out the door and broke into a sprint towards the lift.

The lift door opened on the bottom level, but Triana hesitated. For a moment she remained at the back of the lift, leaning against the wall, grasping the hand railing, peering out into the shadowed gloom. The hallway curved to the left, limiting her field of view to about thirty feet. A heavy quiet greeted her.

Triana's breathing quickened. Her heart banged wildly against her chest, and a thin layer of moisture broke out on her palms. "Calm down," she told herself. "Relax." She swallowed and forced herself to take long, deep breaths.

Letting go of the railing, she took one tentative step out into the hallway. It wasn't simply the faint light that was spooking her, she realized. It was that tomblike silence. A ship this size, with this many people aboard, shouldn't be so . . .

Then it hit her: it was too quiet. The soft background sounds normally supplied by Roc were gone. No wind. No crickets. Nothing.

She paused with her hand across the door sensor, preventing it from closing, using the light that streamed from inside the lift to see as far as possible. What she wouldn't give right now for a simple flashlight. Straining, she listened for the sound of a footstep, a voice, even the sound of breathing.

Nothing.

For a moment she considered calling out. But somehow that seemed creepy, too. No, the intruder had said to meet her on this level. Well, she was here. Time to go find him.

"I can't stand here all night," she finally thought. "Time is running out."

She left the comfort of the lighting within the lift and took a few more tentative steps into the gloom. Her feet padded slowly along the corridor, barely making a sound, while the deafening thud of her heartbeat echoed in her ears. She worried that the pounding might obscure any sound that would alert her to the stowaway's presence. Her breathing was in control now, but the sweat on her palms had not let up.

Brief thoughts of turning back darted into her head, and at one point she actually came to a halt, just before the bend of the hallway. Should she backtrack and call the other Council members? Suddenly this idea of the private meeting did not seem so wise after all.

Shaking her head, Triana took a few more steps. As she rounded the turn she ran through a mental review of this level. Five sealed Storage Sections, inaccessible to the crew—but not to their guest, it would seem. Several more hallways branched off from this main artery. The Airboarding track was at the end of one of these branches, dark and deserted now. Farther ahead, towards the end of the main corridor, were the Spider bays. A large observation window loomed just outside the entrance to the bays, the window that Peter Meyer had sought before his encounter with the intruder. And finally, at the end of the main hall, an emergency stairwell.

There was something else on this level, however, that hadn't occurred to her until now. Something that she had forgotten about. Something that should have registered from the beginning. Something that suddenly clicked.

She saw it as she finished rounding the turn. There, at about waist level, was the access panel to *Galahad's* computer controls. The entry point to the massive electronic brain they lovingly called Roc.

And the panel was open.

She stared at it, trying to comprehend what she was seeing, unaware that she had been holding her breath until it escaped from her in a rush.

There had been no answer from Roc in her room. The comforting Earth sounds were missing. A new, stabbing fear, different from the others that had been crowding her mind, shot through her in a flash. Damage to the ship's computer brain could spell disaster for the entire crew. Roc controlled almost every function of the vessel, including . . .

Including life-support control. Gravity. Heat. Air.

There was still no sound. Her eyes now accustomed to the murky darkness, she cautiously stepped towards the open access panel. As she dropped to one knee to inspect it, more details made sense.

Peter had seen the intruder at this spot. He had told Triana that it seemed as if the man had just stood up. Peter wondered if he had been kneeling. Of course. Opening the panel would require that.

Gap had found the coin at this spot. Somehow that was connected, too.

Triana looked first at the panel as it hung from its hinges. It wasn't as if security at this site was a priority, but Dr. Zimmer still had insisted that it take a special tool to open this section.

There were only two of these tools that she knew of; one in her possession, another with Gap. Who might have a third?

Next, she peered inside, wishing once again for a flashlight. Nothing looked out of the ordinary, but her computer classes seemed like eons ago. What had happened here?

Triana had become so preoccupied with the open access panel that she never heard the quiet footsteps approaching from behind. So focused was she on the problem at hand that the voice, when it came, brought a scream to her lips and a chill to her blood.

"Well, hello, Triana. I wondered if you were going to make it."

That was followed by one of the most hideous laughs she had ever heard in her life.

34

Opening the window didn't do much good, since the air was still and dry. There was no breeze to ventilate the house. After being locked up for several weeks it was definitely hotter inside than out, and Wallace Zimmer thought that any exchange of air would help reduce the heavy feeling that hung within the walls. He leaned against the windowsill and gazed out at the quiet street. The usually bustling neighborhood was subdued, as people sought refuge inside from the stifling late summer conditions. Even the birds had decided to call it quits for the afternoon, as if it required too much energy to muster up even the smallest chirp.

He had lived in this house for almost twenty years. Or, rather, he had owned the property and listed the address as home, even though he actually spent more time away than here. During the two years of overseeing *Galahad* he could count perhaps ten nights that he had slept in his own bed. His neighbors were gracious, keeping his lawn in passable shape and stopping in to make sure everything was in order. One thing he was sure of: never take great neighbors for granted.

He was struck by another coughing attack. This one was more severe than most, and the pain in his chest radiated out to his arms this time. More blood collected in his mouth, too much to swallow this time, and he leaned forward to spit it out the window. Thank goodness the neighbors didn't have to see that, he thought.

No sooner had he collected himself from the attack when another spasm wracked him, more violently than the first. Another mouthful of blood was ejected onto the rocks outside his window, and a tear seeped out of one eye. The pain was becoming unbearable. It was time for another dose of the cough suppressant he had picked up from his doctor this morning, wasn't it? Had it been long enough between doses?

Did that even really matter anymore?

He trudged into the kitchen as mild aftershocks of coughs rippled from his chest. He decided he didn't care if he was an hour or two early for the next dose. All he could think about was stopping the pain. Just stop the pain.

He unscrewed the cap on the medicine, ignored the spoon lying next to it, and tipped the neck of the bottle into his mouth. Two quick swallows began coursing through his system, and within a minute he felt the pain subside. He rested one hand on the kitchen table and the other on his forehead, gathering his strength. This couldn't go on much longer. And, sadly, he knew it wouldn't.

Eventually he pulled out a chair and sat, then slowly replaced the cap on the medicine bottle. The table was littered with books and papers from the *Galahad* project, along with an assortment of e-mails and letters from the families of the kids who had made the trip. Each one thanked him again for the opportunity he had given their child to survive. Each one wished him well. Each one was, in its own way, another good-bye.

He flipped through these notes absentmindedly, looking at them without really seeing them. After reaching the bottom of the stack he started to sort through them again before catching himself and pushing the pile aside. The house was quiet, and lonely.

The sound of the tone from the vidscreen on the table was soft, but still caused him to jump. He checked the incoming call and saw it listed as F. Bauer.

Connecting, he smiled when he saw the face of Dr. Bauer's wife, Sharee. She looked weary—that look was commonplace these days—but managed to smile back at Zimmer. He had only met her on a few occasions, but had instantly decided that she was one of the truly warm, caring people in the world. Fenton Bauer had been very blessed.

"Hello, Sharee," he said.

"It's good to see you, Wallace," she said. "How are you?"

"Oh, I'm all right, I suppose. A little tired. You look as lovely as ever, of course."

Her smile brightened slightly. "You're sweet, but I don't feel lovely. Not anymore. And you know what? I hate to say this, but I don't even try anymore. The way I figure it, this is how I look, so the world better just deal with it. I've retired my makeup bag for good."

Zimmer laughed. "I like your attitude, Sharee."

"Well, it's not like I'm out dancing every night. In fact, I haven't left the house in the last week except to go to the store. Never thought I'd be the type to turn into a hermit, but . . . but I can't really bring myself to socialize much anymore."

"I understand," Zimmer said. In his own mind he wondered if he would venture out very much in the coming weeks, and quickly decided that the answer was no. He had no friends around to speak of. And besides, he didn't feel very sociable himself. What was left of his enthusiasm had launched inside a giant spacecraft and was headed towards a distant star. No, he would probably become just like Sharee, he thought.

"I understand that you'll be writing a book on *Galahad*," she said. "I think that's a terrific idea. Fenton told me as much as he could, but I'd very much like to see it all through your eyes."

"Well," he said, a touch of sadness entering his voice. "I meant to start it a long time ago, but there just wasn't any time before the launch. Maybe now that I'm home . . ." His voice trailed off.

"I'm sorry," Sharee said suddenly. "Of course, you need some time to rest and . . . and . . . and get your strength back."

Dr. Zimmer rubbed his fingers on the kitchen table, feeling a coughing spasm that was beginning to well up. He didn't want Sharee to see that, so he stayed silent for a moment, trying to suppress the attack. She obviously took that to mean that she had said something wrong.

"Listen, Wallace, let me know if there's anything I can do for you. I know I'm clear across the country, but if there's anything I can send to you, or . . ." An idea suddenly occurred to her. "Or maybe you'd like to fly out and stay with us for a little while. We could all go out and do something together."

"That would be very nice," he said. "Although I'm sure Fenton has seen enough of me over the last two years. He'd probably prefer to spend some quiet time with you, don't you think?"

"Maybe," she said, with her own sad inflection now filtering through her voice. "But he hasn't been in a hurry to get back yet."

Zimmer's fingers stopped sliding along the tabletop, and he stared into the vidscreen. "What do you mean?"

Sharee shrugged. "I mean he hasn't made it home yet."

"What? He left the station weeks ago."

"I know. He called me the night before he left, and told me that he felt terrible and was coming home. But he said that he wanted to stop off at my parents' cabin to see if he could convince Marshall to come home."

Dr. Zimmer remembered the many conversations he'd had with Dr. Bauer regarding Bauer's reclusive son. He recalled the pain that was evident each time the topic came up, and the way Bauer had seemed to envy Zimmer's closeness with the crew of *Galahad,* perhaps wishing for that same relationship with his own son. Dr. Zimmer had always been at a loss for words at those times, but on one occasion had asked if a reconciliation was possible. Dr. Bauer had shook his head slowly, but had not answered.

Zimmer stared intently into the vidscreen. "And you haven't heard from him since he went to Tahoe?"

"That's just it," Sharee said. "Marshall's here. He's been here for five days now. And he says Fenton never called or showed up there."

"And you haven't heard anything from him?"

"Nothing. I've been so anxious for him to get home. Marshall's almost like a new . . . well, a new man. He's wanting to reconnect with his father. I think he knows that there's not a lot of time left, you know?" Her weak smile dissipated, leaving almost a grimace on her face.

Zimmer didn't respond.

"Anyway," Sharee said, "when your e-mail for Fenton came in here a couple of days ago I was a little surprised. It sounded like you thought he was here, and I was kind of hoping that he was with you. So I decided to call."

"I'm sorry," Zimmer said. "I . . . I thought he was home. He never said anything to me about going to find Marshall. All he told me on the station was that he was going home." He paused briefly, thinking. "I'll make a few calls," he finally told Sharee.

"I appreciate that, Wallace," she said. "I'll check back with you tonight. Maybe we can figure out where he is. I'm sure there's a simple answer."

Dr. Zimmer wasn't so sure, but smiled at Sharee Bauer and wished her well before breaking the connection. He sat still for a while, his mind replaying the conversation. So Fenton had told him that he was leaving the space station and going home. He told his wife that he was stopping in Tahoe to meet with their son, to try to patch up things. Yet he had never showed up at either location. Nor had Sharee or Zimmer been contacted regarding any type of accident or emergency.

The scientist was missing.

35

Sudden fear can trigger chaos in the human body. A quick, unexpected jolt of fear can instantly double or triple the heart rate. Muscles can immediately tighten, bringing on a feeling of paralysis. Breathing becomes rapid and choppy, palms become sweaty and all of the body's senses shoot into overdrive. The brain scrambles for information, looking for anything to help it recognize the threat and develop a reliable solution to that threat. The survival instinct sends adrenaline rushing through the body, preparing every part for the action needed to protect itself. Yet, ironically, it can also cloud the judgment of the brain, inducing an action that might not be appropriate for the situation or could even make matters worse.

Triana Martell was experiencing all of the symptoms of sudden, crushing fear. The unexpected voice, and the evil laugh that followed it, caused her to immediately freeze, down on one knee, one hand resting on the floor, the other just inside the open panel on the wall. Sweat broke out on her forehead and her palms; her breath came in quick gasps. Her body had tensed, her brain sending out the genetically programmed "fight or flight" response. Triana's initial reaction was to jump up and run. But a split second before getting to her feet, her training kicked in.

Dr. Armistead had spent almost a full week working with the crew of *Galahad* on one particular emotion: fear. She hadn't pulled any punches, either. "There will be times that the slow buildup of fear will weigh upon you," she had told them. "The anxiety you'll feel is only natural; you're all taking on a mission that nobody would have even imagined three years ago. That type of fear can wear you down, exhaust you. We'll cover the types of exercises and meditations that can relieve the stress.

"We'll also teach you to deal with sudden, unexpected emergencies that can provoke a sensation of fear that will almost paralyze your body. You have to be ready to deal with these emergencies without panicking. Nothing is foolproof; some of you will be able to adapt better than others. But all of you will have a fighting chance with the right preparation."

Triana had found that particular stage of their training fascinating. They learned about the amygdala and its effects within the brain. They practiced techniques to slow the body's breathing, which controlled the heart rate, which in turn allowed the brain to better process the rapid influx of data. In short, they learned to overcome the paralysis of abrupt fear. Dr. Armistead had stressed to Dr. Zimmer that it could very well be the training that ultimately would save their lives.

Triana summoned the knowledge from that training as her heart and mind threatened to race out of control. She consciously exhaled slowly, to a count of three, before drawing another breath and letting it out again to another count of three. She felt her heartbeat gradually calm. Taking one more deep breath, she pushed herself back up onto her feet, and turned. In the dim twilight of the corridor she came face-to-face with the intruder.

She was sure that the shock of recognition and surprise was plainly visible on her face, which caused the man to laugh again. The laughter, although quiet, seemed to reverberate through her brain. This was madness.

"Dr. Bauer," was all she could manage to say.

"Triana," he said, drawing out each syllable of her name. "Surprise, surprise, surprise, eh?"

She didn't answer. Her mind was trying to make sense of

what she was seeing, and it wasn't making much progress. Dr. Bauer's usually smooth face was covered with a ragged beard, and his eyes, normally such a warm brown, seemed darker now and tinged with red. His hair was matted and greasy, his clothes filthy and in disarray. From what she could gather in the dim light, the face underneath the beard looked thin and sunken.

Triana's gaze drifted down to Dr. Bauer's left hand, which clutched a long, pointed object. It took her a second to recognize it as the special tool needed to open the computer access panel. She had one stashed in her room; it made sense that Dr. Bauer would have had one as well.

But right now he brandished it more like a weapon than a tool. Triana eyed the sharp steel point with the special hatch marks, designed to fit into the grooves of the panel almost like an old-fashioned screwdriver. Although it wasn't designed to inflict injury on a person, she knew that it was more than capable of tearing flesh. She looked back into Bauer's eyes.

"I didn't think you were coming," he said, the evil grin still beaming. "I almost had to start without you."

Triana swallowed, forcing herself to take another deep breath and exhale slowly. "And what are you starting?"

"The slow death decay of *Galahad*," he said, laughing yet again, this time louder and longer than before. Triana knew now why Peter Meyer had freaked out upon hearing that sound. It conjured up every image of terror that she had ever known, blended with something else that made it even more powerful: a feeling of confidence. Dr. Fenton Bauer had not only set out to destroy the ship and all of its crew members, he was also deadly certain that it was going to happen.

"Tell me why," she said, shrewdly trying to take a step backwards to open up a bit more space between them. Dr. Bauer would have none of it, and moved to his left just enough to block any escape for Triana. She was cornered. Any jump she made could be cut off in a flash, and the sharp point of the tool would bring her down instantly. One more time she cursed herself for braving this meeting alone.

"There are about seven billion reasons that I can think of," Bauer said. "Every man, woman and child that you left behind on Earth. Each person who will have to not only suffer the pain of Bhaktul Disease, but the thought that you get a free pass. A free pass on their credit, too. You see, none of you on this ship stopped to think about that now, did you? That your escape from that disease was actually paid for by the people who will ultimately die from it. What did they get out of it? How do they profit?"

Triana was listening to him, absorbing his warped logic, and trying desperately to find the words to debate the issue. He apparently had a lot to say about the mission, and any chance to engage him in a discussion would hopefully buy more time for someone to stumble onto them. That wasn't likely, she was sure, but worth the chance. She knew her words were important. Angering him might only cause him to react quickly and violently; she had to appeal to him intellectually. He was, after all, a scientist, and would likely want to explain his position, almost as if he were proving a theorem. She had to hope that logic could overcome the insanity brought on by Bhaktul.

"They profit by knowing the human race goes on," she said, measuring her words carefully and speaking in a soft, slow voice.

"Ha!" he said with a shout. "You sound like Dr. Zimmer. In fact, that's almost a direct quote from him. I should know; I heard it hundreds of times over the last two years. I expected more from you, Triana. You're intelligent. But now you're coming across as nothing but a trained parrot, mimicking your master. Aren't you able to think for yourself?" He punctuated his remarks by waving the long metal tool in her face. She didn't flinch.

"I'm very capable of thinking for myself," she said. "I've thought a lot about it. And whether I was included or not, I would still have voted for this mission. Mankind has always overcome obstacles, and we won't just pull the curtain closed on thousands of years of progress because of one fluke astronomical event. Even one hundred years ago we wouldn't have been able to do anything about it. Today we can, and we choose to preserve the species."

"More Zimmer nonsense!" Bauer shouted. "You've been brainwashed, girl, that's all. Tell me why you should go? What makes you special?"

This gave Triana pause. There was something underneath his ranting, something that was registering at the outskirts of her mind. Something that told her that Dr. Bauer wasn't necessarily against the mission itself, but rather . . . what? When he spoke again, she understood completely.

"Why should you go, or Gap, or Lita, or any of those other kids? What about all the other kids who deserved a chance to go? What about the kids who were just as smart as you, maybe smarter, who didn't get the chance? Just because some kids were a little older . . ." His voice broke for an instant, a sob that tried to well up but was suppressed. His maniacal waving of the weapon stilled, and he grew quiet.

Triana took a chance. "You're talking about your son, aren't you?"

Dr. Bauer fixed his gaze on her, bloodshot eyes that crept from deep within his sunken face, eyes that bored through her, mixed with hate and madness. She had hit the mark, and knew it instantly.

"My son is better than you or anyone on this ship," he said barely above a whisper. "He's smarter than you, braver than you, stronger than you. He should be here, not back on Earth awaiting a death sentence."

Now Triana had to tread lightly. "How old is your son?" she said, although she knew the answer.

"Dr. Zimmer would tell you that it doesn't matter. He's too old, he would say. But he's not. He hasn't shown one sign of

Bhaktul. Not one sign. He would have called and told me, I know. But I haven't heard a word from him. He's fine, I tell you. There's nothing that should have kept him from this mission. Nothing." He paused, then said, "He would have called me. He would have called."

Triana could have explained that it simply wasn't possible for everyone to go. She could have explained that once children reached the age of eighteen their bodies were able to carry the disease, whether they showed symptoms or not. She could have said all of this. But Dr. Bauer knew it. He knew it but was unable to accept it right now. Whether it was the disease working on his mind or overpowering grief or a combination of both, he wasn't able to admit the truth. Stating the obvious might stall him, but it also might trigger an attack. She instead opted to console him.

"I think you're right," she said. "I'd like to know more about your son. What's his name?"

Bauer sighed. "His name is Marshall."

"Where does he live?"

"He . . . He lives . . ." Bauer's eyes had dropped from Triana's. When he looked up again, lines of sadness were creasing his face. "It doesn't matter," he said. "None of that matters anymore."

Triana realized that time was running out. She tried desperately to think of another line of discussion, but before she could say anything, Bauer took another step forward.

"Nothing matters anymore," he said. "I'm going to end this mission now. Tyler wanted me to finish it back at the space station, but it's better to do it here, now, when there's no one who can step in and help."

Tyler! So Triana was right about one thing. Tyler Scofield might not have been able to sneak aboard *Galahad*, but he had orchestrated this from the beginning. He had been able to infiltrate Dr. Zimmer's organization, working Dr. Bauer into a position of trust, and manipulating him for more than two years.

That explained a couple of things: The beard, for one, and the coin, Scofield's symbol of opposition.

"What are you going to do?" Triana said, attempting to ease down the corridor slowly, inching along to her right.

"Not much, really. But enough to do the job. We were sure to put most of the control of *Galahad* into the hands of the computer." He laughed again, which seemed to drag him out of his funk. "That was my doing, actually. We could have put more control into your hands, but I convinced Dr. Zimmer that you shouldn't have any more pressure on you than necessary. His soft spot, actually. There wasn't much convincing to do there.

"So now I finish disabling your computer, and *Galahad* will begin to drift out of control, and at the same time grow colder and colder. It won't be long until this is nothing but a giant lifeless icebox, gliding throughout the stars forever."

Triana shuddered. The madman's vision was entirely within his grasp.

"And how funny that all it takes is this," Bauer said, holding up the tool he had used to open the access panel. "And this," he added. In the fingers of his other hand he held up another coin, identical to the one that Gap had discovered. Dr. Bauer twisted it back and forth, showing both sides to Triana, basking in her wonder.

"Don't understand?" he said. "It's so simple. So simple, in fact, that if Zimmer only knew what was happening it would crush him."

Here was the delay that Triana had hoped for. Dr. Bauer was indeed ready to explain his plan for destroying *Galahad,* and it pleased Triana for two reasons. First, she needed the extra time. Second, she was curious to find out how an outdated coin was the key to the damage.

Bauer flipped the coin once, twice, then held it up again for her to observe. "I was the one who worked closely with Roy Orzini and Dr. Mynet on the design of your computer. Roy might have been the one who designed the actual brain of the machine, but I was the one who approved the design of the access panel behind you. That's something that Roy and Mynet couldn't have cared less about; they were only concerned with the function of the computer. How it fit into this panel was unimportant to them. But it was vital to Tyler and me.

"All it took was one set of switches. I laid out the panel so that these particular switches would sit right next to each other. Nobody bothered to notice that these two switches, should they come into contact with each other, would slowly feed enough electromagnetic juice through each other to eventually fry the entire system. Since they were welded down inside the panel, nobody ever worried about them coming into contact. But the design was perfect. All it left was a gap about the size of . . . well, the size of this," Bauer said, displaying the coin once again. "This slides neatly into place, and within minutes your computer power will drain away to nothing. Tyler was good enough to furnish me with the metals information, and together we have designed a series of switches that would not do well at all with a bridge made from copper, nickel and manganese. And, what do you know? Those are precisely the ingredients in our friend here." The coin gleamed, even in the dim light.

"But you've already done something to Roc, haven't you?" Triana said.

"Oh, sure. That was nothing. Just a little memory chip, nothing to cause damage. A little something to keep him preoccupied, so he won't know what's coming, and can't send out a warning once the decay begins. It's like a tranquilizer for computers. Or a sleeping pill, maybe. I'm afraid your lovable computer friend did not take to it very well. Not very well at all. In fact, I believe he's grown very quiet." Bauer smiled wickedly. "Probably trying to figure out what's happening to him. But once the coin is in place, it will soon be all over.

"It's a most ironic ending, wouldn't you agree?" he said. "*Galahad*, the greatest sailing ship ever conceived, with a price tag well into the tens of billions of dollars, yet brought down by a piece of metal worth exactly twenty-five cents."

Another short laugh escaped his lips, but now the effect wasn't as chilling. Instead it brought anger to the surface in Triana.

"You tried to insert that once already, didn't you?" she said, again hoping to buy some time. "Someone interrupted your plot the other day, and you dropped your quarter. Why did you wait so long to try again?"

"For one thing, I wasn't going to do it that time. I just wanted to see how long it would take to open the panel with this," he said, indicating the tool. "Remember, I wanted to let you scoot away from Earth before I did anything. And, to tell you the truth, it actually became kinda fun this last week, watching all of you shaking in your boots. It was almost as if I were a ghost on this ship, and haunting you kids was a kick."

He took one more step towards Triana and the open panel. A short spasm of coughing made him pause, a brief look of pain coursing across his face. Then it passed, leaving the wild look in his eyes that had greeted Triana just minutes ago.

He had now drawn to within five feet of her, and pointed the sharp tool towards her face. "And now, enough talk. Please have a seat right there while I finish my work. This shouldn't take long."

A million thoughts screamed through Triana's mind. If she let Dr. Bauer insert that coin, it meant the end of the mission and the deaths of all 251 crew members. If she struck out at him, he would easily overpower her and then just finish the job anyway. She decided to take the risk. In her mind there was simply no alternative.

She inched along the wall again, keeping her eyes on his, waiting for the perfect opportunity to strike. Bauer's eyes flitted back and forth between her and the open panel at about knee level. As soon as he was within reach of it, he pointed the tool at her throat and took another quick glance down. At that exact moment, as he prepared to drop to one knee, another severe coughing fit took hold of him, and he reflexively closed his eyes. Triana did not waste the gift.

Her foot shot out and made direct contact with Bauer's wrist. It brought a yelp of pain and forced his arm backwards. But, to Triana's despair, he kept a firm grasp on the weapon. She jumped and kicked again, this time with a blow to his chest. The large man staggered backwards, his shoulders colliding with the corridor wall, his head banging solidly. A surprised look appeared on his face, but it was short-lived, quickly replaced with a grimace of rage. With a shout, he braced one arm against the wall, preparing to push off in a wild charge at Triana. She tensed her muscles, ready to repel the attack, her eyes drawn to the sharp metal tool that Bauer raised above his head.

36

Tyler Scofield was humming a song, one of his old favorites, a song taught to him by his grandmother. She had tried to teach him the words, but apparently had a hard enough time remembering them herself, because each time they came out in a slightly different form. Tyler hadn't cared; he loved the melody and knew enough of the words to sing a short chorus, which satisfied him. His grandmother had told him about the days of actually buying music in stores, something that seemed quaint and ridiculously old-fashioned. "Thank goodness I never had to resort to that," he had told himself, thankful for the ability to search for and secure any music, of any generation, within seconds.

His humming was the soundtrack to his afternoon in the sun. He was alone on the deck of the cottage, two miles from the nearest village, overlooking the Sea of Cortez. The town of Loreto, along the Baja strip of Mexico, was just a short ride south whenever he needed supplies. That wasn't very often. He was content to wait out his final days in total isolation, a recluse now after a lifetime of civilization overload.

He had loved the drama involved in dropping out of sight. Each time a newscast carried a story of his disappearance, he chuckled. It made no sense to him why anyone should want to keep up with his whereabouts, especially now that *Galahad* was gone and the human species was preparing to enter the home-stretch. He had said all he needed to say over the past two years. What more did they need to hear? What did it matter where he chose to spend his final days?

Looking out across the dark blue water, he spied a fishing boat. The crew appeared to be moving about as quickly as he was this afternoon, which made him wonder how they got anything done. One man stood nonchalantly at the wheel, barely moving, and another was quite obviously asleep, sprawled back into a chair with his feet up on the railing. A large, floppy hat shielded his face from the blistering late afternoon sun. A third man sat near the stern, lazily tending to a tangled net, but not appearing to be in any hurry to get it straight. He would occasionally lean back and spit something into the water, then refill his mouth. Seeds, probably sunflower seeds, Scofield imagined.

Watching the slow trek of the boat made him think briefly about another ship that had sailed. This one was full of teenagers, and its speed was considerably faster than the fishing boat's. It would be approaching the speed of light within a year, creating the first real test of Einstein's theories regarding space flight and time distortion. Too bad there wouldn't be anybody around on Earth to measure the results.

Too bad, also, that the ship had sailed in the first place. Scofield had given everything he had to prevent the mission from succeeding, including diplomatic pressure and public pressure. He had even gone so far as to plant a saboteur within Wallace Zimmer's inner circle, someone who could short-circuit the plans from inside. Fenton Bauer had not been Scofield's ideal choice, but at the time it was difficult to be picky. It was easy enough to find someone who was adamantly against the mission; finding someone who could do something about it and remain quiet was a stiffer challenge. Scofield had wondered about Bauer's dependability, but ultimately had given the green light. Unfortunately, he had failed.

Watching the fishing boat and its three sleepy keepers make

their way towards a rocky point, Tyler Scofield made a sudden decision to contact Zimmer. He had read his rival's e-mail a couple of days ago, admiring the class of the man if not his ideals. It couldn't hurt to make one call. He could hide the location and maintain his privacy.

Punching in the code, he waited, sipping from a bottle of water, and noting the drift of the boat around the point and out of sight. Just when he thought he was out of luck, his vidscreen came to life, the face of Wallace Zimmer staring back at him.

"Tyler? My goodness, the entire world seems to be looking for you."

"And yet you're the only person I bother to call, Wallace. How are you?"

"Tired. Weary, I guess, is a better word. Weary from the physical and mental drain. Plus our friend Bhaktul has come to call."

"I'm sorry," Scofield said with a murmur.

"Oh, it's in the cards for all of us. I'm just thankful I was able to finish . . ." Zimmer broke off the sentence.

Scofield detected the awkward feeling and put the scientist at ease. "Yes, of course. That was more than two years of extremely hard work. And it's partly the reason for my call. First off, I'd like to thank you for your sincere note. It's a shame that we were at odds these past couple of years. But I want you to know that our differences never affected my respect for you. We . . . we agreed on the problems, just not always the solutions."

Zimmer stared silently into the screen.

"Listen, Wallace, as much as I desperately tried to kill your project, I'm afraid that you were the better man. Consider this a call of congratulations. I might have objected to your plan, but I appreciate the skill and grace that you brought to it. You've achieved something that, three years ago, I would have thought impossible. Kudos to you, my old friend."

Zimmer seemed touched. He nodded at his adversary. "Thank you, Tyler. Your call means more to me than any other note I've received. That's the truth."

"I don't believe we'll be hearing from each other again," Scofield said. "I just thought you deserved to hear this. Believe me, I tried as hard as I could to keep this from happening. If you only knew."

A look of concern came over Zimmer's face. He hesitated before speaking up again.

"Please do not take offense at this, but I do have a question about your . . . campaign to disrupt the *Galahad* mission."

"Yes?"

"Is it possible that you had someone working on the inside of the project?"

Scofield remained stoic, staring into the vidscreen. "Why do you ask?"

"Well . . . it's actually bothered me from the start. I would spend many nights lying in bed, thinking of everyone who came into contact with the project, wondering if they could all be trusted. I believed that our security was as good as could be expected, but still . . ." Zimmer rubbed his chin thoughtfully. "Still, how can one ever be completely sure, right?"

"Right," was all Scofield could think to say.

"Here's the reason I ask," Zimmer said. "There hasn't seemed to be any major problem with *Galahad* since she left. The last time I checked with Tracking, they said all seemed well. But now . . ."

"What is it?" Scofield said, sitting up straight.

"There are a couple of things that have me concerned. About two hours ago I received a call from my office. *Galahad* has gone silent. They can't seem to raise the main computer, which could be a minor issue. Besides, it's only been a couple of hours. Could be any number of reasons.

"But I've been doing some thinking this afternoon. Since the launch, two people have dropped out of sight. The call from you is reassuring, since you were one of them. The other person is Fenton Bauer."

"What do you mean?" Scofield said.

"I talked to his wife yesterday. She hasn't seen him since he left the space station two weeks ago, just before the launch. Nobody has heard from him."

Scofield sat still. A strong breeze began to blow in from the water, ruffling his hair and adding to the chill that had enveloped him in the last minute. At first he thought of admitting everything to Zimmer; then he decided against it. But after another moment he changed his mind yet again. What could it hurt to talk now?

"Wallace, this news is . . . well, it's very troubling. You know how adamantly I was opposed to this project from the first day you proposed it. And, yes . . . I did try to sabotage your efforts from the inside. Fenton Bauer was my best chance."

Scofield could see the shock written on the face of his old friend. He hadn't expected that look to cause such pain in his own heart, but the realization of betrayal brought a heavy feeling of shame upon Scofield, as if he hadn't played fair. He quickly explained.

"But we failed, Wallace. Do you understand? Fenton and I were working together to cripple the project, that's true. But once *Galahad* launched I gave up."

"I don't understand," Zimmer said. "What were you doing?"

"It was all in the computer, that amazing computer you installed aboard the ship. Our plan involved frying its brain on the eve of departure. We knew that it was an integral part of the ship; in fact, we knew it couldn't function without that computer. And destroying it the day before launch would mean a complete retrofit, something that would take months, and probably not get approved. We were counting on public opinion to swing our way if you suffered a defeat like that, and it would spell the end of *Galahad*."

"But . . . ?"

"But Dr. Bauer was unable to get to the computer access panel like we had planned. That computer genius of yours, Orzini is it?"

"Roy Orzini."

"Yes. We didn't count on him staying aboard the ship until the very last moment. I guess he wanted to babysit that child of his right up until the launch. Dr. Bauer tried everything possible to sneak in alone, but there was no opportunity. So instead he called and informed me that he was leaving. I presumed that our last hand had been dealt, and it was a loser. Disappointing, extremely disappointing. But not completely unexpected. I never figured to have better than a fifty-fifty chance of winning."

"And Dr. Bauer? You've not heard from him?"

"Nothing. He simply said he was leaving the space station. I assumed—like you, I suppose—that he was going home."

Dr. Zimmer seemed to digest all of this. If Bauer was in league with Scofield, and had missed his chance to disrupt *Galahad*'s computer . . .

"I think he's aboard the ship," Zimmer said.

"What? How could that be?"

"I don't know, Tyler, but I'm sure of it. That's why we haven't heard from him, and now we've lost track of the ship."

"Wallace, you must believe me. It's true I tried to wreck the launch. But I would never support anything that might harm any of those kids. My God, I was trying to save them from the beginning!"

"I'm starting to see a portrait of a different man than you or I knew," Zimmer said, his voice cold. "You might not have sent him aboard with the intention of killing anyone. But it's possible that that's exactly what you've done. Intentions don't matter anymore. It's very likely that you encouraged a man who is unstable. And I place the responsibility of the lives of those 251 kids on your shoulders, Tyler."

37

Triana braced herself for the attack.

Suddenly a shout came from behind her. Dr. Bauer froze, and both of them looked down the corridor towards the lift. Around the corner stepped Gap, Lita and Channy. Their faces displayed the shock of recognition, their mouths open and disbelieving.

Finally, Gap spoke. "Hold it, Dr. Bauer. Stop right there."

Bauer's surprise dissipated quickly. With Triana still gazing at her companions in relief, he launched himself towards her and grabbed her around the shoulders with one arm. With the other he placed the sharp point of the tool against the side of her neck. Gap and the others stopped in their tracks, stunned at what they were seeing.

"Not another step," Bauer said. "Triana can tell you that I won't hesitate to use this."

Gap looked back and forth between the crazed eyes of the scientist and the face of the Council leader. If he expected a look of terror in her eyes, he was surprised. She remained calm and quiet. No struggling, no frantic squirming. She looked back at Gap, steady but alert.

"Just let her go, Dr. Bauer," Gap said. "Let her go and let's talk."

"That's ridiculous," Bauer said, slowly stepping backwards,

dragging Triana with him. "This very sharp instrument and Triana's very delicate neck place me in the position of power here. You'll do exactly as I say, do you understand?"

"There are three of you," Triana said firmly. "Don't worry about me. He's trying to—"

"Shut up!" Bauer tightened his grip on her, his left arm coming up under her chin and snapping her head back. It cut off the sound from her throat, but her eyes kept their steely stare. Bauer took another step backwards, his breathing getting heavier and heavier. Triana wondered if another coughing attack might strike, giving her the chance to wriggle free.

Instead, from behind, came another shout.

A hand crashed down on the right arm of Dr. Bauer, sending the tool to the ground, where it spun a couple of times and came to rest. Triana fell forwards against the wall, reaching out with her hand at the last second to prevent herself from slamming face-first into it. The impact brought her down to one knee, and she turned to see what had happened.

Dr. Bauer had recovered, and was wrestling with Bon. Triana couldn't believe the sudden change of fortune. Where in the world had Bon come from?

Gap, Lita and Channy were suddenly at her side, helping her to her feet. As the four of them turned to help Bon, Bauer gained control in his fight and, grabbing Bon by one arm, viciously slung him into the other Council members. Without hesitating, the scientist took off in a scramble down the corridor.

"Tree, are you okay?" Gap said.

"I'm fine. Bon, thank you. You—"

"He's getting away!" Bon said. "C'mon."

"He can't hide anymore," Channy said. "Let's get some more help down here—"

"No, there isn't time," Triana said suddenly. "He's heading for the Spiders."

"What?" Channy said as Triana, Gap and Bon began sprinting away. She turned to Lita. "But he's trapped, right?"

Lita looked back at her with a grim expression. "If he's able to take off in one of the Spiders, it could be very bad news." She began to run after the others, while the consequences dawned on Channy. A madman, loose in one of the Spider craft. And a target like *Galahad* waiting like a giant bull's-eye.

Bauer covered the short distance to the Spider bay doors in seconds. Rushing into the large hangar, he managed to close the door behind him, buying just a few more seconds. By the time the others were able to reach the bay and reopen the door, he had scrambled inside the nearest Spider and sealed the hatch.

Gap was the first to reach the Spider, but was too late. The hatch was locked. Slamming his hand against the side, Gap screamed through the glass. Fenton Bauer, strapping himself into the restraints, responded with a laugh. Within seconds a flashing strobe light cut across the room, along with a warning siren.

"C'mon!" Triana shouted. "We've got to get into the Control Room before he opens the bay door into space. This room will depressurize in seconds!"

The five barely made it into the adjoining Control Room before the warning siren intensified and one of the Spider bay's outer doors began to slowly open. They sealed the Control Room, watching through the large window as stars became visible through the round Spider bay opening. Bauer had control of his vessel and started the conveyor belt that would glide the craft outside *Galahad*. In thirty seconds the Spider reached the gaping hole. The last thing the Council members saw was Bauer, laughing hysterically as the small ship dropped through the opening and was gone.

"This is not good," Lita said. "Now what can we do?"

"Two things," Triana said. "First, Gap, get back to the computer access panel and get to work on Roc. I don't think he's damaged too badly. There's a chip that's been installed. Get it out of him, and get him restarted."

Gap shot out the door of the Control Room into the corridor and ran back towards the panel. The moment he was gone Triana turned to Lita.

"I need you and Channy to get back up to the Conference Room and wake the rest of the crew. Let them know what's going on, and get them ready for a collision."

The two girls took off, leaving Bon and Triana alone in the room. He looked out the window at the hangar just as the bay door closed and the room began pressurizing again. The empty space where Spider #1 had been sitting seemed odd. The other nine Spiders sat gleaming before their own bay doors.

"Now what?" Bon said.

"I'm thinking," Triana said, chewing her lip and looking at the remaining escape ships. Only eight were completely fitted for life support to begin with. Now they had seven for a crew of 251. The two others sat mutely by themselves, their doors draped with multiple warning signs.

"For now," Triana said, "go help Gap. I want to get Roc up and running as quickly as possible."

Without a word, Bon turned and left.

Triana flipped on the vidscreen beside her and punched in the tracking program. In a moment the screen converted to a black grid. The large shape of *Galahad* sat in the middle. To one side Triana could see the flashing blip that represented the missing Spider as it moved away. According to the scale it was already dozens of miles away. But it was slowing. Triana felt her muscles tighten again. This was bad.

At the access panel on one knee, Gap scoured the inside of the computer's central control. He had found and removed one chip that certainly didn't belong, and was looking for others when Bon arrived.

"Well?" Bon said.

"I don't know. I want to make sure I've got everything before

I try to fire him back up. It's already going to take a few minutes, and I don't think we have much more time than that."

"What's this?" Bon said, picking the chip off the floor.

"The monkey wrench that Bauer tossed into the works. I don't know what it did to ol' Roc's brain, but it sure got his head spinning."

Gap paused during his examination of the computer's interior and looked at Bon. "By the way, you were right about coming down the emergency stairwell. I thought you were nuts, but I've got to hand it to you. You surprised the daylights out of Bauer by sneaking up behind him."

Bon grunted, seemingly uncomfortable with the compliment. "Is there anything I can do here?"

"This is a one-person job." Gap glanced down the hall. "I think you'd better get back to the Spider bay. Don't let Triana do anything stupid."

"Like what?"

"Like take off after Bauer." Gap resumed his search, glancing back at Bon briefly to make sure he understood the implications.

Without another word Bon stood up and sprinted back down the corridor.

He burst back into the Spider Control Room. It was empty.

Looking out the large window into the hangar he saw Triana opening the door of one of the remaining Spiders.

"Triana!" he yelled, then raced into the bay, reaching her as she stepped inside the Spider.

"What are you doing?" he said, grabbing her hand. "Get out of there."

"Let go of me, Bon," she said. "I know what I'm doing."

"I know what you're doing, too. Now get out of there."

Triana took one look at his hand on hers, then back at his face. Her heart began beating a little bit faster.

"Tree," he said, a look of pleading on his face. Triana knew that it was the first time he had ever used the nickname that everyone else seemed to use. After a moment she reached over with her other hand and placed it on his. She felt him get tense.

"Listen to me," she said, her voice soft. "It's not what you think. Just let me go for a minute, okay? We don't have much time."

After another few seconds of hesitation, he allowed her to lift his hand off hers. Before letting it go, she gave his hand a squeeze. Then she was gone.

He watched her through the window of the Spider, climbing into the pilot's seat and evidently starting some sort of prelaunch activities. A minute later she was clambering back out, then sealing the hatch. She could see the confusion on Bon's face as she grabbed his hand and quickly pulled him back towards the Control Room.

"You wanna let me in on this?" he said.

They entered the Control Room and sealed the door. Triana sat at the console and began to make adjustments.

"They weren't able to finish all of the Spiders before we left. Two of them were really just put aboard for spare parts. But they still fly."

Bon looked out the window at the Spider she had been in. It had the warning signs posted on the door. A look of realization crossed his face. "You're going to fly it by remote control."

"That's right," Tree said. "It can't support life inside, but it will work just fine as a robot ship."

Bon looked at the vidscreen showing Bauer's craft. The distance between the scientist and *Galahad* was now closing.

Triana noticed the look of alarm on his face and nodded. "Yeah, he's started on a collision course. Since he couldn't finish the job from the inside, he's gonna try it from the outside. He'll ram us and that will be the end of it. This ship might be big, but it's a little too delicate to handle that."

Suddenly a tone sounded. It was Dr. Bauer, calling from the rapidly approaching Spider. Triana wasn't sure if she wanted to talk with him, but then realized that it might keep him occupied for the brief time she needed. She punched the intercom.

"Hello, kids," Dr. Bauer said. His voice sounded strained and high-pitched. Triana realized that the last of his control had withered away. He was now completely insane.

"Just wanted to say good-bye . . . again," Bauer said, adding the laugh that had already chilled Triana a few times. "According to my calculations—rough calculations, of course—you have about three minutes left. That's not much time, is it?"

Triana listened to the words but blocked out the message. She needed all of her concentration as she worked the computer controls in front of her. Bon stood beside her, quiet but attentive. He shifted his eyes back and forth between the vidscreen that was tracking Bauer and Triana's efforts. In a flash of realization he understood exactly why she had been selected as the Council leader. This was undoubtedly the most stressful, fearsome moment of their lives, and she was working with utter calm and determination.

Dr. Bauer's voice drifted out of the speaker again. "Nothing to say?"

"I'm sorry for you," was all that Triana said in reply.

"Sorry for me? You're sorry for *me*? I am doing exactly what I set out to do. Maybe not the way I planned it, but it doesn't matter. This ship should never have left Earth."

He continued to babble, but by now neither Triana nor Bon was really listening. With the final calculation complete, Triana engaged the firing sequence. The two Council members looked up through the window to watch the outer bay door swing open in front of the empty Spider. A wash of starlight seeped in, then was blocked momentarily as the escape craft taxied out the opening. In seconds it was away, leaving the doors to close slowly behind it.

Looking back at the vidscreen, Triana and Bon were able to track both of the Spiders. Dr. Bauer continued to hurtle towards *Galahad,* but now their robot craft began to accelerate on its own collision course. Triana kept her gaze on the converging blips, Dr. Bauer's hurtling along at a blazing speed, her own robot challenger barely beginning to gallop. With one hand she made a barely perceptible adjustment to the robot Spider's course, while the other goosed the throttle on its rocket power. She knew she had to be perfect; she had one shot, and one shot only. A miss meant the end.

"One minute, kids," Dr. Bauer said.

As he was saying this, Gap entered from the corridor and stood in the doorway to the Spider control room, listening. Neither Triana nor Bon sensed his presence, and their backs were to him. Gap started to speak, but wondered if it would disrupt whatever Triana was working on. He held his tongue, his hands opening and closing into fists, sweat beginning to trickle down his forehead. He heard Bon say something softly to Triana, something that sounded like "Has he noticed?"

Triana flipped off the intercom and answered clearly. "No, I don't think so. He hasn't adjusted his course at all." She made one final course correction, then let go of the controls.

With that, Gap figured out what was happening. He held his ground in the doorway, awaiting the outcome.

A moment later he watched Bon's hand slowly reach out and take Triana's. She held on to it firmly. Gap's mouth dropped open silently.

"Twenty seconds to collision," Triana said. "He's bound to discover it any moment now." She flipped the intercom back on. "Oh, Dr. Bauer?"

"Yes," he said, his voice even more sinister. "This is . . . wait. What—?"

He had finally discovered the oncoming Spider. But by now it was too late. Triana and Bon, their hands clasped even tighter, watched his incoming craft suddenly begin to veer to one side, but it wasn't able to maneuver that sharply. On the vidscreen they saw the two points of light clip each other, then branch off at severe angles. Apparently the impact had not been dead-on, but rather a glancing blow. Would it be enough to send Bauer's ship skidding past *Galahad*?

The intercom gurgled, cutting in and out, the connection damaged. Triana thought she could hear Dr. Bauer coughing, then silence. A moment later came what sounded like a sharp cry, then silence again.

Seconds later the blip of Bauer's Spider careened past *Galahad*. Bon would later estimate that it had likely missed their ship by no more than fifty feet. It spun wildly, damaged beyond control, and shot away into the void of outer space. For a few seconds the radio connection became clear again, and in that brief moment both Triana and Bon were sure of what they heard. It was Dr. Fenton Bauer, laughing. It was enough to chill their blood. Then his voice, now much lower and heavier, broke through.

"You won't make it, kids," he said. "It's a long way to Eos. You don't have what it takes to make it. You never had it." The signal broke up again, sputtered back to life briefly, then faded. The last thing they heard was Dr. Bauer repeating, "You won't make it. Just wait. You won't make—"

Then he was gone.

Triana and Bon relaxed their grips, then turned and looked at each other. Simultaneously they reached out for each other and hugged, pulling themselves into a tight embrace. They remained that way for a long time.

By the time they parted, Gap had quietly slipped out of the doorway. He began to trudge back down the corridor, past the open computer access panel and on to the lift.

38

A thunderstorm crackled overhead. The wind had picked up with the storm, whipping the trees and slamming the rain into the side of the house and the windows. The power had gone off almost ten minutes earlier, and Dr. Zimmer wasn't hopeful that it would be restored anytime soon. He wasn't even sure that anyone would bother to find the problem. It might be the next morning before his lights came on again. Which was fine with him.

It was close to midnight and why did he need a light anyway? He lay still in his bed, an empty bottle of cough suppressant on the nightstand. He had drained the last third of it in three large gulps, knowing full well that it was dangerous to down that much of the strong medicine in one sitting. But he just didn't care anymore.

His conversation with Tyler Scofield had sapped whatever passion remained in his life. He felt defeated, betrayed and help-less. Another call to Sharee Bauer had depressed him further. But he had decided to not confess his suspicions to her. Why bur-den the sweet woman with the guilt when she had no control over the situation? Instead he had consoled her as best he could over her missing husband, and had promised to stay in touch.

He wouldn't be staying in touch, of course, and they both knew it. Yet it had seemed the proper thing to say. Sharee had smiled at him, one tear tracing down her cheek with many more ready to follow, as her image faded away on his vidscreen.

Now he listened to the storm, his house and the rest of the neighborhood swallowed up in the darkness. The brief flashes of lightning illuminated his room through the windows, allowing him to see a framed photograph on the opposite wall. In it, a smiling Wallace Zimmer sat on the front row of the bleachers at the *Galahad* training facility. Around him were gathered the 251 pilgrims selected to journey forth amid the stars. A look of pride, mixed with sincere love and affection, beamed from his face. And there was another look, as well. It was a look of gratitude. For this group of kids had given him—for two years, anyway—a family.

As he closed his eyes, he realized that the pain was subsiding. The already dark room began to recede further into inky blackness, and the sound of the storm gradually faded away. With one last breath, he prayed that his family was okay.

39

Twelve hours had passed since the encounter with Dr. Bauer. The weary Council members sat slouched in their chairs in the Conference Room. Each had spent a couple of sleepless hours in their rooms, their adrenaline keeping them charged throughout the rest of the night. By morning they had managed to doze for an hour at most, then awakened and cleaned up enough to stagger into a Council meeting.

Triana was at the head of the table, looking around, a faint smile on her lips. Lita returned it with her own grin and reached out to squeeze Triana's hand. Tears returned to Channy's eyes, the emotion of the incident still evident on her face. Bon fiddled with his cup of water, occasionally throwing a knowing glance at Triana, but for the most part maintaining his standard scowl. Gap sat still at the far end of the table, his hands clasped, unable to keep eye contact with Triana for more than a second or two.

"Roc?" Triana said.

"Present," came the familiar voice of Roy Orzini.

"It's good to have you back."

"Good to be here. And look, I missed all of the excitement."

"Do you really think we'll ever let you forget about that?" Channy said, wiping her eyes and managing a laugh. "In our greatest time of need, Roc takes a nap."

Lita and Triana joined her in laughing. Bon smiled faintly. Gap remained still.

"Want to know the worst part?" the computer said. "Waking up and the first face I see is Gap's. Holding a screwdriver. Please, Triana, do me a favor, and see if he messed around with my Masego game programming. He could have done anything to me while I was out. Oh," he added, "and while you're at it, check around and make sure there aren't any more quarters on the ship."

"We took Dr. Bauer's quarter, and his wicked little computer chip, and dumped them," Lita said. "And the door he used to get into the Storage areas is sealed again. I was tempted, you know—"

"Yes, I know," Triana said. "I think we all wanted to take a peek inside there. But it's better to seal it off and leave Dr. Zimmer's plan alone. He didn't want us in there, so we'll keep our noses out until we reach Eos."

"I'm also a little worried about a couple of other things, though," Lita said. "What Dr. Bauer said at the end. 'Just wait.' Doesn't that sound like he's done something else to the ship?"

The Council was silent while they thought about that. Finally Tree spoke up.

"Well, we've checked everything that we can. Roc has run through every test he can. Nothing has come up. So, if Bauer did do something, I suppose we'll have to worry about it when—and if—it happens. It won't do us any good to stress out now."

Channy said, "Plus, the man was so far gone, he might have just been trying to scare us again. He might not have done anything."

"Yeah," Tree said. "That's a possibility." She turned to Lita. "What's the other thing you're concerned about?"

"Well," Lita said, "at some point we need to talk about the Spiders."

"Yeah," Tree said. "We're down to eight now, and just seven that will support us." She sighed, looking at the others. "Well, I guess we have five years to figure that out."

Bon spoke up. "That's the kind of stuff we can overcome. I'm not concerned with the Spider situation. But there is something else."

He made eye contact with the Council. "That crazy scientist who almost killed us threw out a pretty good challenge, didn't he? Remember what his last words were? 'You won't make it.'"

The room was silent. All of them stared at the Swedish boy. He looked at Triana, who nodded. Deep inside she hoped that Bon had gained new respect for her as a leader. For some reason, something that she couldn't put into words, she longed for his acceptance above that of anyone else.

She also wondered about their brief time alone in the Spider Control Room. Did that mean anything to him? Would he ever acknowledge it to her? Was he sorry it had happened at all? Or was it just a product of the tension of the moment, never to be repeated? In the aftermath of their near deaths, she was fascinated by her own thought patterns. Rather than reflect on the trauma of their encounter with Dr. Bauer, her heart was pushing her head out of the way. Or trying to, anyway.

Internally she shook away the romantic cobwebs and focused on the point Bon had just made concerning Bauer's forecast.

"I consider that motivation," she said. "Apparently Dr. Bauer never wanted us to succeed in the first place. He figured we would foul up our training, but we didn't. He and Scofield figured they could sabotage the ship and cripple us. They didn't. And Dr. Bauer tried to rattle us so much that we would lose our focus and fall apart. Well, we didn't."

"'That which does not kill you makes you stronger.' Isn't that how the saying goes?" Channy said.

"That's right," Lita said. "And I'd like to remind this crew of something else. We've just confronted a man who wanted us to fail. He was a partner, I guess, with a few other people who also wanted us to fail. But let's remember one thing." She stood up, her hands resting on the table. "There were thousands of other people who gave the final years of their lives to make sure we didn't fail. And millions of others, people we never saw or heard from, who showed their support. So, as hard as it is to imagine, we're really not alone out here, you know?"

She smiled at her friends, then walked out of the room.

Channy stood up, walked behind Triana and gave her shoulders a small squeeze. "I'm proud of you, Tree," she said. "And Lita's right; we're not alone." She turned and started towards the door. "I need to work out. My bones feel tired."

Triana and Bon rose from their chairs and started to leave. Bon walked out, but Triana stopped and looked down at Gap. "Are you okay? You haven't had anything to say. That's not like you."

Gap shrugged. "Just overwhelmed still, I think. I'm all right."

"I want to thank you again for getting Roc back up and running. I don't know what we'd do without you. You know that, don't you?"

"Thanks," he said halfheartedly.

Triana waited another moment in the awkward silence. There seemed to be something hanging in the air between them, and she was pretty sure what it was. But how could she talk about this with Gap right now? All of their emotions were still churning, and she wouldn't know how to approach the subject anyway. She felt for him, knowing exactly what he was experiencing, but reluctant to address it until she'd had time to think about it.

Imagine that, she thought: "the Ice Queen" had two relationship issues to deal with. And she had no idea how she was going to handle either one.

She started towards the door again. "I'll see you in the Dining Room later, okay?"

"Sure," Gap said.

A minute later he rested his head on one hand, a single tear emerging.

"Lita's wrong," he said under his breath. "Some of us are alone."

T errifying and yet beautiful at the same time. Dangerous, but still peaceful.

Triana stood by herself at the large window, holding her notebook and gazing at the inky blackness outside, marveling at the contradictions of space. She wondered how a universe so populated with ferocious, blazing suns could be so very cold.

And she wondered about her place in it all.

Biting her lip, she refocused her gaze from the brilliant backdrop of stars to the reflection of the tall, dark-haired girl who stared back from the glass. Two years ago she was living a dream in the mountains of Colorado. Her father was healthy and happy, and life was . . . perfect?

But now her world was not only upside down, it was gone, dropping farther away behind her every second. Her mother was a stranger, her old friends were memories.

And her father . . .

Not really dead, she decided. She looked into the reflection of the green eyes and for a moment imagined him looking back. Imagined him tumbling out of that raft. Imagined him reaching for her paddle, her dragging him back into the boat, and the two of them laughing. Always laughing.

And she thought about the encounter with Dr. Bauer. He was an incredibly brilliant man. She had been smarter.

He had planned for months to destroy them. She had out-
witted him.

The crew had been on the verge of panic. She had restored
their confidence in the mission and the Council.

She managed the faint beginning of a smile and nodded.
With a flip of the wrist she opened her journal to the day's entry
and added one more line.

Thanks, Dad. Now I know what I got from you.

She turned away from the window and made her way to the
lift, her thoughts drifting from the past to the future. Within a
few weeks *Galahad* would have its final contact with Earth people
when it came into the vicinity of the Saturn research station.

Triana couldn't help but wonder what was in store for them
around the ringed planet.

Let's chat a moment, okay?

I can sense a few troubled looks on some faces out there, so we'd better settle a few issues before Triana and the crew get any closer to Saturn.

First of all, some of you are worried that Dr. Bauer might have done something else to the ship. Some of you are concerned about that whole Spider situation, and what happens when they get to Eos and are short a little transportation. Some of you are going out of your minds that Triana could possibly be interested in a grouch like Bon. All valid concerns.

But let me just say that I'm a little hurt that not one of you expressed the slightest concern about me while I was knocked out. Are some of my chips damaged? Was I scared? Am I going to be the same witty and charming Roc that you've grown to know and love? No, you're more worried about Triana's love triangle with Bon and Gap. Thanks a lot.

Oh well. We'll address the issues which seem to be much more critical to you.

#1: Did Dr. Bauer sabotage the ship some other way?

I can't say; you'll need to read on.

#2: What about the Spiders? Will the crew be able to get down to Eos?

I can't say; you'll need to read on.

#3: What's up with Triana and Bon and Gap?

I'm not stupid enough to stick my computer nose into that mess; you will definitely have to read on.

Besides, if you ask me, there are much more crucial issues at hand. Like the bad feeling I'm getting about Saturn. It used to be my favorite planet, what with those gorgeous rings and everything. Something creepy is bound to happen, I just feel it.

And neither you nor I will know until The Web of Titan.

In the meantime, I've got a lot of work to do.

Excerpt from

The Web of Titan

by Dom Testa

The storm raged quietly along the surface, a swirl of colors colliding, mixing, weaving. Layers of gas clouds tumbled across one another, their brilliant shades of red and purple highlighted by short bursts of lightning. Winds galloped along at more than a thousand miles per hour, stirring the atmosphere and keeping the roiling chaos churning in much the same way it had for billions of years.

Above it all drifted the jeweled rings, chunks of ice and dust that varied in size between grains of sand and ten-story buildings. Their dense orbits stretched out hundreds of thousands of miles, occasionally sparkling like a crown in the dim sunlight while casting a thin, dark shadow across the face of the storms. The tightly packed debris in the rings rolled along, nudging and shoving, forever keeping watch over the unruly gas giant below.

Saturn toiled along.

Scattered near and far, its squadron of moons maintained their dutiful orbits, subjects kneeling before the majesty of the king, tossed about by the immense gravitational tugs and seared by the overwhelming inferno of radiation. Several dozen of these minor bodies drifted near Saturn's dazzling rings, themselves a product of an earlier moon that had been shattered by a rogue asteroid or comet, the pieces now trapped in a mindless dance that circled the giant planet.

Keeping a respectful distance, and shrouded in a cloak of dense atmosphere, the largest of these moons obediently tracked through the vacuum of space, cutting a path that kept it clear of the rings. Dwarfed by the Herculean planet, it still laid claim to its own cloud system and weather patterns. Rather than water, its rivers and oceans were pools of liquid methane, carving channels and shorelines that dotted the surface, a surface impossible to see through the screen of haze and fog. An eerie orange glow masked the surface, bathing it in a dull light that made the large moon almost seem alive, breathing.

Titan.

As it circled Saturn, a route that took it a little more than two weeks to complete, Titan had its own companion in space. Right now, in an artificial orbit, a metallic pod shot around Titan, spinning slowly as it navigated, the light from Saturn occasionally glancing off its sides, mixing with the orange tint of the moon to form a ghostly shade. The smooth steel of the pod was uniform except for two small windows on one end, and exhaust ports on the other. During its slow, deliberate trek around the moon, block lettering could be made out on one side, along with small emblems of flags that lined up under a window. Inside it was dark, quiet, waiting.

It would not be quiet, nor waiting, much longer.

Lita Marques sat before the mirror in her room. She deftly tied the red ribbon into a knot, pulling her dark hair into a ponytail and lifting it off her shoulders. She eyed the end result with a neutral glance, then gazed past her own reflection to the smiling girl who sat cross-legged on the end of Lita's bed. "All right, Channy, what's so funny?"

Galahad's Activities/Nutrition Director, clad in her usual bright yellow shorts and T-shirt that made a startling contrast against her chocolate-toned skin, replaced her grin with an expression of innocence. "Funny? Oh, nothing funny." She uncrossed her legs and scooted them over the edge of the bed. "Just wondering why you bother to make yourself look so pretty every day and then refuse to let me set you up with someone."

Lita's eyes rolled. "Why did I bother to ask?" She made one final appraisal in the mirror, then turned to face Channy Oakland. "I appreciate your intentions, Miss Social Butterfly, but I'm perfectly capable of meeting a boy on my own."

Channy raised one eyebrow. "Uh-huh. And quite a great job you've done in that area, too. We've been away from Earth for, what, four months now? Not counting your lunches with Ruben Chavez, you've been out with. . . . hmm, a whopping total of zero boys." She leaned forward and picked a piece of fuzz off Lita's shirt. "And we won't count Ruben. You only talk with him because he's from Mexico, like you."

"Hey, I like Ruben. He's one of the nicest guys on the ship."

"Of course he is. But you know darned well what I'm talking about, and it's not chatting over an energy block in the cafeteria."

Lita shook her head. "Channy, do you think it would be possible for you to go two days without trying to play matchmaker? When I'm ready to see someone, I will. Besides," she added, "I haven't seen you exactly setting the shipboard romance gauge any higher."

"That's because I'm still in advance scouting mode right now," Channy said, winking. "I'm compiling data, see? Give me another few weeks and I'll set the hook."

"Right," Lita said. "Compiling data. I like that." She smiled at the Brit, then stood up and walked over to the built-in dresser and rummaged for a favorite bracelet. The dorm rooms on

Galahad were relatively small but comfortable. Each crew member shared their space with a roommate, but the work schedules were usually staggered to the point that each person was able to have time to themself, a valuable commodity on a ship loaded with 251 passengers. Lita, one of *Galahad*'s five Council members, was responsible for overseeing the ship's Clinic, or Sick House, as it was lovingly referred to by the crew. Her roommate, an outgoing fifteen-year-old from India, was currently at work in the Engineering Section. Channy had stopped by to accompany Lita to dinner.

Finding the accessory she wanted, Lita slipped it over her wrist and turned back to face Channy. "Let me ask you something," she said. "Are you as curious about our upcoming appointment at Titan as you are about my love life?"

Channy shrugged. "Of course. I'm just not sure exactly what we're doing. I asked Gap about this . . . this pod thing we're supposed to pick up, but he was pretty busy at the time and never really explained it to me. And good luck getting a straight answer from Roc about anything."

This brought a laugh to Lita's lips. "Oh, he'll shoot straight with you eventually. What exactly do you want to know?"

"Well," Channy said, "if this pod is supposed to have been launched by the scientists on the research station orbiting Titan, how come we haven't heard from them? Nobody seems to be saying much about that."

"Yeah, it's a little creepy," Lita agreed. "Thirty scientists and engineers, all working for a couple of years on a lonely outpost near Saturn, and suddenly nobody can get in touch with them." She walked over to the desk across the room and called out to the computer. "Roc?"

"Hello, Lita," came the very human-sounding reply. "What's on your mind?"

Lita couldn't hear the computer's voice without seeing the short, lovable genius who had programmed the machine. Roy Orzini, one of the champions of the *Galahad* project, had been responsible for outfitting the ship with a computer capable of controlling the life-support systems, lights, gravity and other crucial functions of the spacecraft. As a bonus he instilled an actual personality into the thing; *his* personality, it turned out, for the talking computer soon demonstrated the same wit and sarcasm as its creator. Roy's Computer was soon shortened to RoyCo, and eventually to Roc. He was indispensable to the five Council members, almost an older brother along for the ride.

"I'm trying to explain to Channy about the pod we're picking up pretty soon," Lita said. "About the research station that has gone silent. But I'm not sure I really know exactly what it's all about."

Roc remained silent a moment, then said, "Well, if you love mysteries, you should really love this, because it's not just one thriller, but two: the disappearance of the research crew, and this metal pod we're supposed to snatch out of space."

"What's the story on the scientists?" Lita said, sitting down at the desk. "Who are these people anyway?"

"A combination of biologists, medical researchers, engineers and technicians," said the computer. "Maybe not the group voted 'Most Likely to Party in Space,' but all brilliant in their fields. The research station is a small space station in orbit around Titan, the largest moon of Saturn, and one of the most important bodies in the solar system."

"Why?" Channy asked. "What makes Titan so special?"

"Life," Roc said. "Or, at least one of the best chances at finding it off the planet Earth. Titan, you see, has an atmosphere and oceans."

"Oceans?" Channy said. "You're kidding."

"Not the kind you'd want to surf in, my friend," Roc said. "These are oceans of liquid methane. But bubbling around in that poisonous soup are a lot of the building blocks that eventually led to life on Earth billions of years ago. This research station has been studying Titan for several years."

Lita picked up a stylus pen from the desk and tapped her

cheek with it while she listened to Roc. Now she paused and said, "What have they found?"

"That's just it," said the computer voice. "All of their reports have been labeled classified and top secret. Nobody knows what they've found. But apparently, at about the same time *Galahad* launched, something happened around Titan, and all contact with the scientists was lost. The last message was pretty garbled, didn't make a lot of sense. But it mentioned a small pod that was jettisoned into Titan's orbit, waiting."

"Waiting for what?" Channy said.

"Us."

Tor Teen
Reader's Guide

About This Guide

The information, activities, and discussion questions which follow are intended to enhance your reading of *The Comet's Curse*. Please feel free to adapt these materials to suit your needs and interests.

About the Author

Dom Testa grew up a world-traveling Air Force "brat" with a passion for radio. He got his first radio job at the age of sixteen. In 1993, he joined Colorado's MIX 100 where he cohosts the award-winning "Dom and Jane Show." A frequent speaker at schools and libraries, his passion for reading, writing, and education is profoundly evident in his Galahad books as well as his Big Brain Club, a website dedicated to encouraging young people to be proud of their intellectual accomplishments. He lives in Colorado.

Writing and Research Activities

I. Welcome to "Humanity's Lifeboat"
  A. You have just received a letter of invitation to join the
     Galahad project. If you accept, you must leave home to-
     morrow to begin two years of training in hopes of being
     one of the 251 young people chosen for the crew. With
     classmates or friends, role-play a conversation between
     yourself and family members in which you weigh the
     pros and cons of this opportunity.
  B. Write at least four journal entries describing your train-
     ing regimen; your teachers; your emotions at being se-
     lected as one of *Galahad*'s 251 crew members; and your
     assessment of leading students Triana, Gap, and Bon.
  C. Make a list of the five to ten items you will bring to
     decorate your onboard living quarters and remind you
     of home. Be creative and choose wisely. Afterward,
     share your list with friends or classmates and explain
     your choices.
  D. You are looking at your former home planet as *Galahad*
     launches into space. Use colored pencils, oil pastels,
     chalk, or other art materials to draw a picture of what
     you see. Write ten words that describe your feelings.
  E. On page 81, Dr. Zimmer refers to *Galahad* as "humani-
     ty's lifeboat." Imagine you overheard your teacher use
     this phrase. Now, as you sit in your living quarters
     aboard *Galahad*, write a short essay describing what
     this phrase means to you.

II. A Knightly Ship
  A. Go to the library or online to learn more about the
     Knights of the Round Table, the Holy Grail, and Sir Gala-
     had. Based on your research, create an outline, list, or
     fact web of ways in which the spaceship is appropriately
     named. If desired, invite classmates or friends to make

similar outlines suggesting other names, supported by facts about their history and meaning, and vote to choose your group's favorite name for a humanity-saving ship.

B. Can a computer feel? Go to the library or online to learn more about cutting-edge research on artificial intelligence. Use your research to create an informative poster or pamphlet addressing this question.

C. Consider the suggestions made by Dr. Zimmer, Dr. Bauer, and Dr. Orzini about the design of the ship's main computer. Then, divide into two groups to debate the following: The ship's computer should/should not have a friendly personality to support the work of the teens on board. Use library or online research to support your positions.

D. Based on details from the text, re-create *Galahad* in one of the following ways: (1) Draw a diagram of part or all of the ship on graph paper; (2) Create a three-dimensional model using clay, pipe cleaners, or other craft materials; or (3) Use PowerPoint or another computer program to make a "Resident's Guide to Galahad" with animations if possible.

III. Past-Present-Future

A. Research an historic epidemic such as the Great Plague of London (1664–1666) or the Influenza Pandemic (1918). Collect facts about the disease, its effects on society, and how the health threat concluded. Make a two-columned chart on which you compare your research to Bhaktul, the disease of *The Comet's Curse*.

B. Could the events like those described in *The Comet's Curse* come to pass? Why is it helpful to reflect upon such possibilities? Create an annotated list of science-fiction works that make us consider the course of our nonfiction future. You may want to include the novels *Ender's Game* by Orson Scott Card; *The Giver* by Lois Lowry; *Feed* by M. T. Anderson; *The Scorpion King* by

Nancy Farmer; and film/television features such as *2001: A Space Odyssey* and *Planet of the Apes*. If desired, add graphic novels, cartoons, paintings, and other creative works to your list.

C. Create a character guide to *The Comet's Curse*. For each character (human or computer) in the story, write a brief entry describing the character's past, role on *Galahad*, and what you think they imagine their future holds.

D. Role-play the following scenario with friends or classmates: You are the host of a morning radio talk show whose engineer has managed to arrange a connection with *Galahad*'s communication's system for five minutes. Choose the shipboard teen you would most like to interview, prepare your list of questions, set the timer and . . . go! If possible, make an audio or video recording of your interview.

E. Visit http://eospso.gsfc.nasa.gov/ to learn about EOS, NASA's Earth Observing System. Then, write an essay answering the following question: What does EOS teach you about our planet and how does this information affect your reading of *The Comet's Curse*? Or, with a friend or classmate, role-play a conversation between a modern-day student and a student from *Galahad* in which you discuss human life and activities on Earth and in space.

Questions for Discussion

1. After reading only the prologue to *The Comet's Curse*, who did you think was going to be the story's narrator? Were you surprised to discover the identity of the narrator? Did you trust this narrator? Do the other main characters of the story trust this narrator? Explain.

2. What is Bhaktul Disease? How does the presence of the disease affect life and society on Earth?

3. Why doesn't Triana want to look back at Earth as *Galahad* launches? What insights into her character does this choice give readers? Where did Triana grow up? What qualities make her a good Council leader?

4. Why does Wallace Zimmer develop the *Galahad* project? Who are Zimmer's supporters? Who is his most strenuous detractor? If you were a member of the scientific community of this period, do you think you would be for or against Zimmer's work, and why?

5. What is the relationship between Roy Orzini and Roc? In what way does the relationship resemble that of parent and child? How are parent-child relationships a key motif in the novel? How are these relationships important to children? How are they important to parents? What different outcomes result from challenging parent-child relationships in the story?

6. What secret does Channy know about Gap? Does Bon have a similar secret? How do these secrets affect the boys' choices and actions aboard *Galahad*?

7. What does Peter Meyer see in the Storage Section of the ship that dramatically changes the mood onboard? What are the Council members' initial reactions to Peter's outburst? What other strange events follow Peter's outburst?

8. What are Bon, Gap, Channy, and Lita's responsibilities aboard *Galahad*? What qualities resulted in their being chosen for these jobs? Do you think the selection process described in chapter 16 was a good one? Had you been selected for *Galahad*, to which of these roles do you think you would be best suited and why?

9. What is in the Storage Sections? Do you think the plan to keep these sections unopened until the passengers reach Eos is a

good one? Do you think everyone on the crew will be able to resist the temptation of these sealed compartments?

10. What are Roc's thoughts about *Galahad's* mysterious extra passenger? How does he describe the relationships forming between the Council members? How do Roc's insights affect your reading of the novel? If you were aboard *Galahad,* how might you consult, confide in, or play with your computerized companion?

11. Near the end of the novel, how do Dr. Zimmer and Dr. Scofield begin to repair their relationship? How does this lead Zimmer to concerns about Dr. Bauer? What conclusions are Triana and her crew beginning to draw at the same time?

12. What are the other Council members' reactions to Triana's revelation of the mysterious e-mail message? When Triana heads to the Storage Section to confront *Galahad's* intruder, is she completely alone? Explain.

13. How does Triana stall Dr. Bauer in the Storage Section? Who comes to her aid? How does the group work together to defeat their former teacher? How do Bon and Triana work together and what effect does this have on their relationship? How does this affect Triana's relationship with Gap?

14. What is the status of *Galahad* and its crew members as the novel draws to a close? Do you think their mission can continue successfully now that they are aware of Roc's weaknesses? In what way is the crew stronger with this knowledge?

15. Do you think *The Comet's Curse* is foremost a story of the struggle to preserve humanity, or of the power of individual relationships? Explain your answer.

16. Do you think that *Galahad* will make it to Eos? Why or why not? In your opinion, what are the greatest threats or obstacles to Galahad's success?

About the Author

Dom Testa (www.DomTesta.com) divides his time between the spoken and written word. The host of a top-rated radio show in the morning, he turns to writing in the afternoon. His passion for inspiring creativity in young people resulted in The Big Brain Club (www.BigBrainClub.com), which encourages kids to overcome the peer pressure to dumb down. It's also a forum for teachers and parents to express their thoughts on education and literacy.

Dom lives in—and loves—Colorado.

Join Club Galahad!

Be the first to get Galahad updates!

★

Find out about special Galahad events!

★

Links to other great sites!

★

Trivia contests for prizes!

★

You get it all when you join Club Galahad. Just visit:
www.ClubGalahad.com